P9-DFQ-471

JAN    2011

# BLASTIN' THE BLUES

# BLASTIN' THE BLUES

## LOREN LONG & PHIL BILDNER

SIMON & SCHUSTER BOOKS FOR YOUNG READERS
NEW YORK    LONDON    TORONTO    SYDNEY

SIMON & SCHUSTER BOOKS FOR YOUNG READERS
An imprint of Simon & Schuster Children's Publishing Division
1230 Avenue of the Americas, New York, New York 10020

SIMON & SCHUSTER BOOKS FOR YOUNG READERS
is a trademark of Simon & Schuster, Inc.
For information about special discounts for bulk purchases,
please contact Simon & Schuster Special Sales at 1-866-506-1949
or business@simonandschuster.com.
The Simon & Schuster Speakers Bureau can bring authors to
your live event. For more information or to book an event, contact the
Simon & Schuster Speakers Bureau at 1-866-248-3049
or visit our website at www.simonspeakers.com.
Book design by Lizzy Bromley
Hand lettering by Mark Simonson
The text for this book is set in Century 731 BT.
The illustrations for this book are rendered in charcoal.
Manufactured in the United States of America
0110 FFG
2 4 6 8 10 9 7 5 3 1
Library of Congress Cataloging-in-Publication Data
Long, Loren.
Blastin' the blues / Loren Long & Phil Bildner. — 1st ed.
p. cm. — (Sluggers ; [5])
"This is the fifth book in the Sluggers series
(previously published as Barnstormers)."
Summary: In 1899 New Orleans, Louisiana, the Travelin' Nine must
try once again to outsmart the Chancellor, but even the magic baseball
may not help while the players suspect there is a mole on the team.
ISBN 978-1-4169-1867-7 (hardcover)
[1. Baseball—Fiction. 2. Supernatural—Fiction. 3. Brothers and sisters—
Fiction. 4. Spies—Fiction. 5. New Orleans (La.)—History—19th century—
Fiction.] I. Bildner, Phil. II. Title. III. Title: Blasting the blues.
PZ7.L8555Bl 2010
[Fic]—dc22
2009022343
ISBN 978-1-4169-9883-9 (eBook)

To Rebecca Davis,
the glue that holds the team together
—P. B.


To my father,
William G. Long,
who introduced me
to the Big Red Machine.
I'd still rather go to a ball game
with you than anyone.
—L. L.


## ACKNOWLEDGMENTS

A special thanks to David Traxel, author
of *1898: The Birth of the American Century.*
Your writings provided us with our
research launch pad.

# Pregame Recap for
# BLASTIN' THE BLUES

After the waves of activity at the game in Minneapolis and Preacher Wil's stunning debut as the Travelin' Nine's new star pitcher, the barnstormers have little to celebrate. The team just couldn't compete with the Chancellor's dirty tricks and they lost. Ruby and Griffith, while upset over the loss, are flooded with concern over the mysterious old man's words: *There is one amongst you who cannot be trusted.* Is there a spy on their team?

But the game wasn't a total washout. In the eighth inning Graham experienced a strange occurrence when he somehow stopped time and saw his father. Was it a dream? Or is it, as Graham fervently wishes, a sign that his dad will return for his birthday?

Hoping to leave their troubles behind them, the barnstormers boarded the train to their next game in St. Louis. But a surprise attack from the Chancellor's men sent Dog, Griffith, and Woody jumping from the train to save their magic baseball from the thieves. Can the team be reunited in time for their next game? And can the Travelin' Nine find a way to get back on a winning streak before it's too late?

# Contents

The Chancellor's thugs stood just yards away.

# 1

★

## *Walking the Dark Tracks*

"**Don't say a word,**" Woody whispered, his finger pressed to his lips. Griffith nodded once. He could feel his heart beating in his chest. With a trembling hand, he gently stroked the back of Dog's head. The Chancellor's thugs stood just yards away, and the faithful hound refused to stop his purrlike growling.

Under the cover of darkness, Griffith, Woody, and Dog huddled together in the thick brush by the side of the tracks. After leaping from the speeding train bound for St. Louis, Woody had used the skills he'd honed fighting in the jungles of Cuba to steer them to this patch of high grass. So long as they remained silent and motionless, they would be safe.

Griffith looked up. Even in the pitch dark, he could make out the shapes of the Chancellor's thugs. He was able to hear their every word, too.

"We need to get out of these woods," one said.

"We need to find that baseball," said a second. "Boss man's gonna—"

"We're never going to find it out here!" the third thug cut him off. "I ain't staying in no woods all night."

"Boss man's going to have our necks when he learns we don't got it."

"That dumb dog got it." The first thug kicked at the ground.

Griffith covered his eyes from the spray of pebbles and dirt, while Woody leaned over and shielded Dog.

"I reckon city thugs ain't the same animal

2

as wilderness thugs," Woody mouthed. He rubbed Dog's hind leg, the one he had hurt jumping off the train. "We're gonna be fine, Griff. Let's just wait 'em out."

Griffith nodded. He rubbed the scrape on his elbow, the only injury he had suffered from the leap.

"I ain't looking for no mutt out here," the first thug went on. "We'd run into a wolf or a bear wandering these woods."

"Boss man's going to be furious we didn't get the kid."

"To heck with the kid and that ball!" The first thug kicked the dirt again. "Too late to do anything about either one. Might as well go back now before some creature comes along."

The Chancellor's men headed off. In a matter of moments, their voices and footsteps could no longer be heard. Still, Griffith, Woody, and Dog remained in their hiding spot.

"If you ask me," Woody said softly as the minutes passed, "they're long gone." He rubbed the bruise on his cheek. "But I reckon we're gonna hold our position a little while longer."

Despite Woody's assurances, Griffith didn't believe they were entirely safe. The Chancellor's men could still be lurking in the woods, preparing to pounce. He tried to tell himself that Dog would've been growling if they were, but it didn't help. And the constant rhythms of the tree frogs and crickets, and the periodic hoot of an owl, also kept him on edge.

He ran his hand through his hair. The Chancellor's men had tried to *kidnap* Graham. Griffith had known the Chancellor was capable of anything, but in his worst nightmares, he'd never thought the Chancellor would order his thugs to try to *take* his little brother. The goons had tried to steal the baseball, too. They'd ripped it away from his sister. The Chancellor had instructed grown men to rough up a young girl.

Griffith slipped his still-trembling hand into his pocket and gripped the baseball. The attack had taken place more than an hour before, but he wondered if he would ever stop shaking.

"I still can't believe you jumped off that train," Woody said, as they headed down the tracks.

"I can't believe you jumped off either," Griffith replied, flinching as a rabbit or raccoon darted across the rails.

Woody smiled. "I wasn't about to leave you behind. A soldier never leaves another behind."

"It wasn't like I was alone. I had Dog with me."

Griffith reached down to pat the hound's

head, but the shriek of a bird caused him to recoil again.

Dog drifted over and brushed his snout against Griffith's pants. As they walked along, the canine favored his left hind paw. At times he raised it off the ground and used only three legs. Griffith wondered if Dog would be able to make it all the way back to Minneapolis.

When they'd started walking a short time ago, Woody had told Griffith and Dog that they would head back to the city. At the time they'd leaped from the train, they couldn't have traveled more than ten or twenty miles. While it would be a long trek, one that would more than likely take all night, it was the safest course of action, since they had no way of knowing if the next town was five or fifty miles ahead.

"You still worried 'bout them bandits?" Woody asked.

Griffith didn't answer.

"Well, I ain't gonna tell Griff Payne not to worry, because I know that won't do any good." Woody chuckled. "I reckon we focus on something else. Like that baseball. I'd like to see it."

Griffith reached into his pocket for the ball and handed it to Woody. Cradling it with both hands, the Travelin' Nine's right scout held the sphere to his face and examined it as closely as he could in the darkness.

"I've only held this treasure in these here hands one other time," Woody said. "And believe it or not, I was walkin' the tracks just like this."

"Where was that?"

"Before heading off to Cuba, most of us were stationed in Tampa, Florida." Woody spoke softly and deliberately. "Thousands and thousands and thousands of soldiers all in one place. We Rough Riders came in from San Antonio, but by the time we arrived, them train tracks was so clogged with freight

SCOUT: *outfielder. The right fielder was called the "right scout," the center fielder was called the "center scout," and the left fielder was called the "left scout."*

7

cars, we had to get out and finish the journey on foot. Walked the tracks like we are now." Woody tightened his grip on the baseball. "It was durin' that walk that your pop let me hold this here baseball. The only time he did. And you know what he said to me?"

Griffith shook his head.

"Your pop made me a promise, Griff. Promised me my life. Promised all the Rough Riders our lives. Said we'd all return from Cuba." Woody lifted a hand from the baseball and raised a finger. "But he said there was one condition. You know what that was?"

"I do," Griffith replied, smiling.

On many occasions, his father had told him what he'd said to his fellow soldiers before heading off to war. They were the same words he so often said to Griffith and his sister and brother.

"Be together," Griffith said, gazing up at Woody. "Always."

Woody ran his fingers over his smile, then placed the baseball back into Griffith's hand.

"Uncle Owen gave us the baseball the night of the funeral," said Griffith, slipping the object back in his pocket. "He told us not to tell anyone we had it."

"I figured that's when y'all got it," Woody said, nodding. "But some of the others didn't think it showed up till Louisville or Chicago and—"

**BARNSTORMERS:** *team that tours an area playing exhibition games for moneymaking entertainment.*

"Wait," Griffith interrupted. "All the barnstormers knew we had the baseball?"

"'Course we knew!" Woody laughed. "We've known for some time. But we was all too amazed at how well you kids could keep a secret to say anything. A seven-year-old boy, a nine-year-old girl, and an eleven-year-old boy all kept their mouths shut." Woody laughed again. "Now, that's magic!"

Griffith thought back to the exchange

he'd had with Happy in the dugout during the game in Minneapolis. Happy knew about their baseball; he'd made that perfectly clear. But what Griffith hadn't realized was that *all* the Rough Riders knew about it too. There was no need for secrecy when it came to the baseball (especially after what had just taken place on the train), and for the first time since the attack, Griffith felt a hint of relief.

He looked ahead and squinted his eyes. They had to have been walking for at least a couple of hours now, but the faint glow of lights from the city still didn't appear to be getting any closer.

"I reckon there's a bigger secret we need to deal with on this team," said Woody. "Scribe and I have been talking about it, and we're concerned that—"

"There's a mole on the Travelin' Nine," Griffith interrupted again.

Woody stopped. A wooden railroad tie

cracked underfoot. "How do you know?"

Griffith could see the anguish on the Rough Rider's face.

"It's the only thing that makes sense," Griffith answered. "Ruby thinks so too." He swallowed. "And that's what the old man told us."

"The one you spoke about in the dugout?"

Griffith nodded. "We didn't want to believe it, but once the old man said what we were thinking, we couldn't deny it. It hurts so much to . . ." His words trailed off.

"It sure does," Woody said. "I reckon it's a hurt like I've never experienced. Never." He started walking again. "On the one hand, I'm so angry I want to grab this man by the throat. But at the same time, we're talking about one of us, a brother who served by our side in the war. It's heartbreaking." Woody pinched the bridge of his nose. "How can a member of your *family* betray you like this?"

Griffith frowned. It was as if Woody was speaking Griffith's own thoughts. And Ruby's, too.

*There is one amongst you who cannot be trusted.*

The old man's words echoed in Griffith's head.

"How are we going to figure out who the mole is?" asked Griffith.

Woody sighed. "It could be almost anyone."

"How do I know it's not you?"

Woody stopped again.

Griffith gasped. He couldn't believe that question had just left his lips. How could he be so disrespectful? But as he started to wish the words back, he caught himself, because a part of him was glad he'd been courageous enough to ask.

"I reckon you don't know it ain't me," Woody said. He turned to Griffith and rested both hands on the boy's shoulders. "But I offer you my word, Griff. Your pop made a promise to me, and I make a vow to you." He paused. "I am a man of honor."

Woody wasn't the mole. Griffith was certain. But it was more than merely his words that told Griffith that.

*Some things you just know.*

Griffith turned and looked up at the tracks. The moonlight reflected off the rails, two white lines pointing the way back to Minneapolis.

"We're gonna be spendin' a whole lot of time together these next few days, you and I," Woody said, draping an arm over Griffith's shoulder as they started walking again. "I reckon you're gonna get to hear all my war stories." He let out a short laugh. "Heck, by the time we make it to St. Louis, you're gonna know just 'bout everythin' that went on down there in Cuba."

"I'd like that," Griffith said. He reached down to Dog and stroked his neck. "I'd like that a lot."

In the past, Griffith's father had tried to tell him stories from the battlefield, but Griffith had always made him stop. The only tales he was able to tolerate were the ones from San Antonio, when the Rough Riders had first met. Griffith didn't want to know about those days without food and water and those nights without sleep. Nor did he want to hear about all the brushes with death.

But that was before this summer. Now Griffith needed to know absolutely everything. What happened in Cuba could very well contain some of the—

Suddenly Dog's ears perked up. The hound glanced around and then gazed into the night sky, his eyes appearing to follow something in flight.

"What is it, Dog?" asked Griffith.

For a brief instant, he thought he saw the outline of a moving object, but it quickly disappeared.

As dawn began to break, Griffith, Woody, and Dog finally reached the city limits. Because of the eerie fog hovering over the metropolis, the lights of Minneapolis had never seemed to get any closer as they walked back. But now daylight had brought the city into full view, and Griffith began to recognize some of the buildings, streets, and signs. He even spotted the bridge they had walked across on their way to the match in Nicollet Park.

**MATCH:** *baseball game or contest.*

However, when they neared downtown, Woody steered them from the tracks.

"Where are we going?" Griffith asked. "We need to go to the station to catch a train."

Woody shook his head. "I reckon you can't board a train without a ticket," he replied.

"And how you comin' up with a ticket if you don't have any money?"

Griffith gulped. "I forgot about that."

"I didn't." Woody pointed ahead. "Let's see if we can find ourselves a friendly face or two."

Woody was leading them back to the university. Perhaps someone they'd met at the dorms or the library was still there. Maybe they'd be willing to provide them with food, a place to wash, and money for train tickets.

As they turned up the road leading onto campus and headed for the quadrangle, Dog held his head high. He recognized the spot where he and Griffith had played catch a few days earlier. Soon he was prancing, almost as if he was trying to tell the boy that his hind leg was completely healed. But Dog wasn't ready to play. He was still limping, more than ever. Like Woody and Griffith, Dog needed rest.

Griffith peered in the direction of the dorms. Through the early morning fog, he spotted a figure standing by the front entranceway. He appeared to be staring back at Griffith, almost as if he was expecting a visitor. Griffith approached the silhouette, and the fog thinned, revealing the familiar and unforgettable face.

"Now look what I've done."

# 2

★

## Recovery and Reality

**lizabeth pulled Ruby** and Graham closer. "For so long, I didn't want to believe that the Chancellor was behind all this," she said. "Now look what I've done."

"You didn't do anything," Graham said, squeezing his mother's hand.

"You can't blame yourself," added Ruby. She dabbed the tears from the corner of her mother's eye with the napkin that had been sitting on the table.

At the far end of the dining car, Scribe stepped through the doorway. Crazy Feet and Tales followed close behind.

"We searched every car," the Travelin' Nine's massive center scout announced. "The Chancellor doesn't have any more of his men on this train." He waved to Bubbles and Doc, standing guard by the far door, and pointed them to the tables in the center of the coach. "Let us sit and collect ourselves."

Preacher Wil and Happy shifted over so that there was room for all the barnstormers to sit next to one another. For a few moments, they huddled together in silence. Everyone was still reeling from the attack that had taken place only a short time ago.

"Do you think they found shelter?" Tales finally ended the quiet.

"What if they're hurt?" the Professor asked.

"What if the Chancellor's men found them?" Bubbles added.

Graham squeezed his mother's hand again. Sitting against her, he could feel her tension growing with each question being asked. He looked over at his sister. Ruby was sensing it too.

"Woody's with Griff and Dog," Graham spoke up. He glanced to Preacher Wil as he mentioned the hound. "He'll keep them safe."

Ruby looked back at Graham. Even though he was the youngest of the group and the target of the assault, he was the voice of reason and reassurance. She was stunned by her little brother's cool calm.

"I have all the confidence in the world in Woody," Doc agreed.

"The Chancellor is behind everything," Elizabeth blurted. She gazed around at the barnstormers. "That's what I was telling

Griff when the attack happened. All the
money must be owed to him."

"I'm not so sure about that," said Tales.

"I am," Elizabeth insisted.

For the first time since the raid, Elizabeth
let go of her two children. She stood up and
began explaining to the Rough Riders the
truth about the debt. Like Tales, Bubbles and
the Professor didn't want to believe what they
were hearing, and they tried a few times to
refute her statements. However, when she had
finished spelling everything out, the remaining holdouts could hardly deny the harsh
truth: The debt belonged to Uncle Owen,
not to Guy Payne. The debt was owed to
the Chancellor, which was why his men had
attacked them.

"I didn't allow myself to believe it either,"
she said, directing her words to those most
reluctant to accept what she was saying. "I
didn't want to believe what my own son was

trying to tell me." Her voice was riddled with guilt. "If only I'd listened to him . . ."

"It's not your fault, Mom," said Ruby, reaching for her mother's hand. "You know it's not."

"Mom, you're trying to protect us," Graham added. "You're doing a great job."

"Your children are right, Elizabeth," Scribe said. "Listen to them now."

"If anyone's to blame," Bubbles said, "it's Owen Payne."

But Elizabeth shook her head. "I should have listened to Griff. My son is in danger because of me."

"Griff's fine, Mom," Graham assured her. "He's with Woody and Dog. They're all looking out for one another. I promise."

Graham lowered his eyes. On the floor by his feet, he noticed a black hat that belonged to one of the goons. It must have fallen off during the skirmish. He reached down for the hat and placed it on his head. It was too big, and when he lifted the brim from his eyes, he was met with many disapproving looks. Graham removed the hat and placed it in his lap. He would try it on again later when the others weren't around.

"I need to listen to you kids more," Elizabeth said. She sat back down and pulled Ruby and Graham close again. "Much more."

"He's after much more than money," Ruby whispered to Graham, who perched on his bed across the compartment from her. "The Chancellor's after you."

"No!" Graham smacked his cheeks and pretended to be shocked by the news. "He's after me? Thanks for letting me know, Ruby. I don't think I would've been able to figure that out."

Ruby rolled her eyes. "Very funny, Grammy."

She glanced at the door to their sleeping quarters. After the meeting in the dining car, which had lasted for more than an hour, several of the Travelin' Nine had escorted Graham and her back to the compartment. One of the conductors had offered it to them, in light of what had transpired. Even though the train had been searched, and everyone was certain all of the Chancellor's thugs had jumped off, the ballists weren't taking any chances. They vowed to remain by the entrance to the private sleeping area the entire night.

**BALLIST:** *player.*

"I hope they have the baseball," Ruby said, staring across at her brother and wrapping the covers around her shoulders like a shawl.

"Of course they do," Graham assured her, swinging his legs off the edge of his cot. "Dog's catch was amazing! There's no way he was letting go of it after that grab!"

25

"I hope they're all okay," Ruby added.

She squeezed the back of her neck. She and Griffith had promised Graham that on the trip down to St. Louis they would tell him everything there was to know about the men who were chasing them. They would let Graham in on all the secrets. She had to keep the promise, even without her older brother by her side. After seeing Graham handle himself with such poise in the dining car, she owed it to him.

"The Chancellor confronted Griffith," said Ruby.

"He did?" Graham stopped swinging his legs.

Ruby nodded. "Back in Chicago."

"When?"

"The night after the game," Ruby replied.

"You mean the night before we were *supposed* to leave for Minneapolis."

"Yes, Grammy," she said, frowning. "That

night." Ruby sighed. "I've come up with theories about the Chancellor. Griff and I have talked about all of them."

"What are they?" Graham inched forward. "What did the Chancellor say to Griff?"

Ruby reached under her mattress, pulled out her journal, and flipped to the entry she'd written earlier in the week on the train ride to Minneapolis. She then read the three quotes listed under the heading "The Chancellor's Words."

"'That's not all I want,'" Graham repeated. "'You have something else that I want too.' He was referring to me, right?"

"Yes, Grammy."

Graham lay down on his bed. As he stared into the darkness, thought after thought after thought bombarded his brain. All of a sudden, he realized he knew things that not even his brother and sister did. Some of what Ruby proposed as theories—that he was connected to everything and that the Chancellor was setting a trap—Graham knew as *facts*. He didn't know why or how he knew; he only knew that he did.

And the knowledge terrified him.

Graham sat back up and reached for the black hat hanging from the nail above his pillow. Since the others weren't in the room, he could put it on. He pulled the brim down over his eyes, just like the Chancellor's thugs wore theirs, but because the hat was so big, the front covered almost his entire face.

"There's another problem," Ruby said, rewrapping the covers over her shoulders. "One of the Travelin' Nine can't be trusted."

"I know. I heard the old man's warning too," Graham replied flatly. He lifted the brim. "I'm sure there's a mole on the team."

"How do you know?"

"I just know," Graham said. "Like you and Griff do." He dipped his feet into his slippers and shuffled across the dark compartment to his sister's bed. "I don't want to believe it," he added, sitting down beside her.

"I hate thinking about it," said Ruby. "I hate thinking that one of the Rough Riders can't be trusted. How can . . . how can someone so close to us do something so cruel?" Her voice cracked. "Why would one of them want to harm us?"

"Who do you think it is?" Graham asked, resting his hand on his sister's shoulder.

"I have no idea. Do you?"

Graham shook his head.

"I only know it's not Scribe," Ruby said.

"How do you know?"

"He shares some of what he writes in his journal with me," she replied, speaking slowly. "The things I've read, the things he's read to me—it can't be him. He would never have written some of those things if it was." Ruby swallowed. "And like Griffith says, and like you just said, some things you just know."

Graham drew his sister close, and when he did, the brim of his hat brushed against the side of her head. All of sudden, he wanted no part of the hat. It belonged to men who worked for and stood alongside the most evil man there was. He ripped the hat off his head and threw it to the floor. Then he stood up, stormed over to it, and stomped on it with both feet.

"It's about time," Ruby said, managing a smile.

Graham turned back to his sister. "Now I understand why everyone was so upset when I—"

*Knock! Knock!*

Ruby and Graham froze. But then they saw the soothing shape of their mother sliding open the pocket door.

"I heard a commotion," she said. "Is everything okay?"

"Everything's fine, Mom," Graham replied. He picked up the hat, crumpled it into a ball, and tossed it into the corner. "I was just doing something I should've done an hour ago."

"I'm sorry to bother you at this late hour," she said, stepping in and shutting the door. "But since I heard the noise and the talking, I knew you weren't sleeping." She placed the lantern she was holding on the floor next to Ruby's cot and sat down on the end of her daughter's bed. "I need to talk to you."

"What is it?" Ruby asked.

Elizabeth rested her hand on Ruby's knee and gazed down at Graham, now seated on the floor. "We need to have another conversation," she said. She waited for Graham to look up at her. "It's about your father."

"What about Dad?" Graham's eyes widened.

"Graham, I need you to listen to me."

"Is he coming back for my birthday?"

Graham pressed. "Will he be at the party?"

Elizabeth exhaled. "What I'm about to say to you is not going to be pleasant, but I need for you to hear me. Do you understand?"

Graham nodded.

"Your father is dead, Grammy," she said, her voice firm, but warm. "He isn't coming back. Ever. That's what dead means. No matter how badly you may want him to come back, and no matter how hard you wish for him to return, he can't. We must believe he's gone on to a better place, and that he's watching over all of us at this very moment." She looked deeply into her son's eyes. "Do you understand what I just said to you?"

Graham did understand. Every last powerful and crushing word. In all his life, he had never heard his mother speak that way to *anyone*. He knew she didn't do it to be hurtful. She did it because she needed to be heard and understood.

Closing his eyes and pressing his palms against his temples, Graham couldn't stop his mind from returning to his experience during the game in Minneapolis. How could he have imagined something so real?

Maybe because it involved his father?

But he could see his father waving; he could hear him calling, "Happy birthday!" And no matter how many times he tried to tell himself it was just a dream or vision, and no matter what his mother said, Graham couldn't get rid of his lingering doubts. He had done things when time had stopped for everyone else. There was evidence: There had been snow on Griffith's head—snow that *he* had put there; the pitched ball had not passed right over home plate after all—*he* had moved it. Something *had* happened.

"I need . . . I need to go for a walk," he whispered. He stood up slowly. "I need to get some air, Mom."

"I completely understand," she replied. "But I don't want you going out by yourself." She shuffled over to the door, slid it open slightly, and peeked her head out.

A moment later the Professor and Scribe stepped in.

"I'll take a stroll with you," the Professor said to Graham. "If that's okay."

Graham nodded and headed for the door. The Professor followed him out.

"I'm glad you called us in," Scribe said as soon as Graham and the Professor exited. "I was looking for a way to begin a dialogue. I know it's been quite an evening, and the last thing I want to do is burden you with anything more, but I feel it is my duty." Scribe paused. "It's about Owen."

"Everyone believes me now about the money and the Chancellor, yes?" Elizabeth asked.

"Indeed they do," replied Scribe. He

removed his quill from behind his ear and ran the feathered end across his forehead. "It is difficult news to digest, as you can imagine. Some are having a harder time than others."

Ruby stared at the Travelin' Nine's center scout. In the small confines of the sleeping compartment, he looked even larger than usual. Entering the room, Scribe had ducked low through the doorway, and now inside, instead of standing hunched over, he sat on one knee, his elbow on his leg and his chin in his hand.

"Everyone is so terribly disappointed in him," Scribe went on. "None of us can quite believe the danger and harm his poor judgment has caused. I sympathize with him. So does the Professor. We forgive him because he's Guy's brother, but only because he's Guy's brother. If he were not, it would be extremely difficult. Perhaps impossible."

Scribe tucked the feathered pen back behind his ear. "Unfortunately, some of the others . . . Bubbles and Tales are rather enraged. They are not thinking forgiveness, not at the moment. I am hopeful that they will come around, but I am concerned. We need them."

Ruby dabbed the corners of her watering eyes. Scribe was usually a man of few words. She wasn't used to hearing him speak in such a manner. It only added to her fears and worries.

"They will come around," she said, resting her hand on Scribe's knee. "I know you believe that."

"I do, Ruby," Scribe said, smiling. "Nevertheless, I felt it was my responsibility to tell you all that is taking place."

Ruby closed her eyes. Scribe was not the mole. If there was ever any doubt in her mind—not that there was—it had been removed. Scribe would never lie to her. He would never betray them.

"We cannot keep secrets from one another," he continued. "Not in these dangerous times. We need to be a family. We need to be together. Always."

"Why are you following us?"

# 3

★

## The Old Man Speaks

 am here to help you," the old man with the different-colored eyes said, standing before Woody and Griffith on the steps leading into the dorm.

Griffith smiled. The old man's six words were identical to the ones he had uttered to Ruby, Graham, and him outside Nicollet Park the other day.

"Am I glad to see you!" Griffith declared.

"You know this man?" Woody looked to Griffith and then back at the man with the wire-rimmed glasses, unkempt beard, soiled clothes, and bare feet.

"This is the man we were telling you about," Griffith replied. "He's been following us from city to city. Grammy saw him in Louisville, I saw him in Chicago, and then we all saw him in Minneapolis. He's the one who told us about the mole."

"You must be hungry and tired, Mr. Griffith," said the old man. "I've been informed you've traveled quite a long ways." He raised an arm and pointed skyward.

From high atop the roof of the dorm, a large bird peered down. Even through the lingering fog, Griffith could see it was *the* eagle. The familiar flier flapped a single wing in their direction. Griffith nodded. On the long walk back, when he'd caught a glimpse of the object in the sky, he'd thought it was the great bird. Now he was certain.

"I'd like to know why you're following

us." Woody folded his arms across his chest. "What do you want?"

The old man blinked. "Like I said, I am here to help you, Mr. Woody."

Woody's eyes bulged. "How do you know *my* name?"

"You're Mr. Woody, he's Mr. Griffith, and his name is Dog." The old man held his weathered hand out to the hound, sitting obediently between Griffith and Woody. "I know all your names."

"It's okay, Woody," said Griffith. He rested a hand on the Rough Rider's shoulder. "We can trust him."

"Mr. Griffith is correct," the old man said. "I will not bring you harm. I will do everything in my power to help you. I must."

"Look at Dog," Griffith urged Woody. "He trusts him, and you know there's no better judge of character. If this man posed a danger, Dog would've told us."

Peering down at the scrappy old hound, Woody began to nod. Then he slowly uncrossed his arms. "I reckon if you kids all say he's trustworthy, then I ain't about to argue." He playfully shook Dog's snout. "I certainly ain't about to question this one."

"Thank you, Mr. Woody," the old man said. He extended his hand. "The name's Josiah. Josiah Glass."

"It's a pleasure to meet you, Josiah." Woody shook his hand. "I'm sorry if I seemed standoffish."

"No apology is necessary," said Josiah, pinching his wire-rimmed glasses. "You conducted yourself in an understandable and appropriate manner, especially in light of these dire circumstances."

"I reckon we need your help," Woody said, rubbing his weary legs. "We need to get to St. Louis."

"Indeed you do," Josiah agreed. "But the

next train isn't until tomorrow morning."

"There's nothing that leaves today?"

"I'm afraid there is not, Mr. Woody." Josiah raised his hand. "Rest assured, you need not worry about the Chancellor or his army while you're here. They're already on their way to St. Louis. Alas, the morning train is *our* best option."

"You're coming with us?" Griffith asked.

Josiah lowered his hand and ran it slowly through his long beard, until the tips of his fingers rested on his belt buckle. "I will be meeting up with you. Either in St. Louis or New Orleans."

"I reckon you know our schedule?" asked Woody.

"Indeed," Josiah answered. "But Mr. Woody, I know far more than just your schedule. I know more than . . ." He stopped and began to tremble.

"What is it?" Woody asked. He stepped

forward and grabbed the elderly man by the arm. "Are you okay?"

"Mr. Woody, this is the most painful journey of my life," Josiah whispered, his voice quivering. "But it is one I cannot afford *not* to take. I must put a stop to this." He glanced over his shoulder. "Come," he said. He began to walk toward the entranceway. "Let us step inside. You need nourishment. There's food in the kitchen by the common room."

"We're allowed to help ourselves?" Woody asked, as they followed Josiah in.

"It's not much," said Josiah, leading them down a hall. "We'll put together a few simple plates and head across to the library. It will be a good place to talk and eat, so long as we don't make a mess. Then you will rest. You must be exhausted."

In the kitchen, Josiah pointed his three visitors to an oval table in the corner and instructed them to wait while he gathered the food. A few moments later he headed over to them with a service tray of breads, jams, and fruit.

"I'll carry that," Griffith said, standing up and taking the platter from Josiah.

"Thank you, Mr. Griffith," said Josiah. He turned to Woody. "The pitcher on the counter is filled with water. I collected glasses, plates, utensils—"

"Say no more," Woody interrupted. "I reckon I'll grab those."

"Thank you, Mr. Woody. There's even a bowl for Dog."

Josiah led his visitors back out of the dorm and escorted them across the quadrangle to the library where the Travelin' Nine had held their team meeting just the other day.

Stepping into the library, Josiah filled the bowl with water from the pitcher, placed it on the floor, and asked Dog to wait by the front door. He then led Griffith and Woody to the large rectangular table in the center of the circular main room and sat down across from his two guests.

Griffith put down the tray of food on the table and peered around the library. He shook his head. This was the same room the Travelin' Nine had met in, but it looked different. All the desks, cabinets, tables, and chairs were in their usual places, as opposed to Monday, when the barnstormers had pushed the furnishings to the sides. The octagonal windows between the bookcases were providing far more light. Perhaps because it was later in the morning, almost noon. And the main room itself appeared to be much bigger. Maybe because only three of them were here today instead of an entire team.

Josiah finally started to speak. "There is so much I need to tell you. But I do not quite know where to begin." He removed his spectacles, placed them on the table, and let out a long breath. "I suppose I should explain my appearance. Surely you must wonder why I look like I do."

Woody chuckled. "I reckon the thought has entered my mind a few times this mornin'."

"As far back as I can remember," Josiah began, rocking slowly as he spoke, "even as a small child, I always turned away from material items. They never interested me. I saw the temptations that consumed so many others, allowed myself a small taste, and then quickly surmised that such an existence was one I could not lead. I grew to despise the greed and obsession with wealth that permeated the world, and thus chose a different course, an antisocial existence, if you will." Josiah ran his hands down the front of his ragged shirt. "To this day, I still believe this life of isolation was the only path for me. However, I do concede that the reasoning behind my appearance has shifted. It now contains an additional layer, a form of self-punishment."

"Punishment for what?" Griffith asked, between bites of an apple.

Josiah shut his eyes and clasped his hands on the wooden table. "For the evil I created and all that has happened."

"I reckon I don't understand," Woody said, shaking his head.

"I am responsible for the Chancellor."

"How can you be responsible?" Griffith stared intently at the elderly figure across the table. "That doesn't make any sense. You didn't create him, unless . . ." He stopped.

Josiah opened his different-colored eyes. He glanced to Woody, and then fixed his gaze on Griffith.

Griffith swallowed. He knew what Josiah was about to say next.

"Yes, Mr. Griffith. The Chancellor is my son."

Woody tried to speak, but for the moment, he couldn't collect enough air in his lungs to allow for the formation of words.

"I created the Chancellor," Josiah said, reaching for his glasses with trembling fingers. "I led him to believe he had a great destiny, but I was wrong. I wronged my own offspring." Josiah put his spectacles back on, hooking them around his ears. "It is my fault he has turned out this way. Now it is my responsibility to stop him." He paused. "The Chancellor wants your baseball. He will do whatever is necessary to get it." Josiah brought a fist to his chest and gently beat it against his heart. "Mr. Griffith, many years ago that very baseball was a gift to me, a gift from a dear friend. A quite important fellow, I may add. His name was Henry Chadwick, and—"

"*The* Henry Chadwick?" Griffith interrupted.

"Ah, of course you've heard of him," said Josiah, beaming. "How could the eldest son of Mr. Guy not know who Henry Chadwick is?"

"My pop used to tell stories about him all the time," Griffith said. "He said he's responsible for making the game great. He's the founder of modern baseball."

"Indeed." Josiah traced a finger along one of the many spaghetti-like creases that crossed his forehead. "Mr. Griffith, may I hold the baseball? I haven't in years."

Griffith removed it from his pocket and placed it in the old man's cupped hands.

Josiah's eyes watered instantly, and then a single tear ran down his cheek. "We were dear friends for many years, Henry and I," he said, his voice somber. "He gave me this baseball just after the birth of my son. He said he was entrusting it to me, for he believed it held the key to the future of America's new national pastime. He spoke of an age in the not-so-distant future when a young man would come along who would carry the game into the next century and beyond." Josiah brought the baseball to his chest, and like he had with his fist moments ago, gently beat it against his heart. "I thought Henry was referring to my son, that my offspring was baseball's chosen one. So from the time he was an infant, I made my son keep that baseball on the table next to his bed. For his entire youth, I led him to believe that he was the chosen one, and like any good son, he listened to his father."

"And how did you find out he wasn't?" asked Woody.

"Time, Mr. Woody," Josiah answered. "As the years passed, I saw that my son was a skilled ballist with a powerful arm, soft hands, and a steady bat. But by no means was he a unique talent. So I began to have doubts, though I never said a word. I couldn't tell him I was no longer certain he was the chosen one. Nor did I want to believe it. I stubbornly refused to let go of the hope that one day a sign would show me that he was in fact the one." Josiah lowered the baseball from his chest. "More than anything, I wanted to believe the baseball was intended for my child, not the offspring of another. It clouded my judgment. It changed me. This *temptation* changed who I was." Josiah handed the baseball back to Griffith. "It also changed the way I looked at my own son. He felt it too. How could he not? It made him bitter and angry."

Josiah stood up. He removed his glasses again and began cleaning the lenses with his sleeve. Walking over to the doorway where Dog lay sound asleep, he gazed down at the hound and managed a smile. Then he turned back to Griffith and Woody.

"He was such a bright and caring boy,"
Josiah said, his voice wistful. "I sensed he
knew the truth, that he wasn't this meant-to-
be prodigy. However, he never said a word.
Oh, how I wish he had. But more impor-
tantly, how I wish *I* had. I erred. I made an
awful, awful mistake."

"Parents sometimes do, Josiah," said
Woody. "I reckon we ain't infallible creatures."

"That we are not, Mr. Woody." Josiah
returned to the table and sat down. "More
and more strained our relationship became,
but despite the tension, not once did he ever
express a desire to leave his father's side. As
he grew from boy to teenager to young man,
I simply assumed he would remain with me
in the mountains forever." He paused. "But
then came the day when the eagle left baby
Graham on our doorstep."

Now Griffith held up a single finger. At

long last, he was finally going to learn the truth about Graham's abduction.

*There is so much I need to tell you,* Josiah had said.

Gazing back at Josiah, Griffith let out a deep breath, folded his hands, and fixed his stare on Josiah's different-colored eyes.

"I knew that one day I would have to take the baseball from my son," Josiah went on. He spoke plaintively. "When baby Graham arrived, I knew the moment had come." He pointed upward. "That was the first time I ever saw the eagle. Since then, the great bird has been a presence in my life. In so many ways, he has become a most loyal friend, not merely a messenger or conduit to the outside world."

"We saw him walking back," Griffith noted.

"Indeed you did, Mr. Griffith," said Josiah. "That is how I knew to expect you. I learn much from this trusted companion. The eagle told me when he first encountered you on the steamship."

"The *Meriwether Lewis*," Griffith whispered. "He nodded to me that night."

Josiah blinked. "That's why I went to Louisville. Then he informed me you were heading north."

"Chicago," said Griffith. "Does the eagle really *speak* to you?"

Josiah tilted his head. "We communicate in a number of ways. Often the eagle will lead me to the information he wishes to convey. Other times, all that may be required is eye contact, a flap of the wing, or a simple nod. You must remember, Mr. Griffith, most of our interactions take place far away in the mountains, not in urban settings. I've lived in the wilderness for decades, and thus I've grown attuned to the natural world. I understand wildlife, birds in particular." Josiah adjusted his spectacles. "So to answer your question, yes, the eagle does speak to me."

Griffith glanced over at Dog, still sleeping soundly by the door, and nodded thoughtfully. Yes, like the elderly man and the eagle, Griffith and Dog spoke to each other too.

"Enough about the eagle," Josiah said. He wiggled his fingers in the direction of the baseball protruding from Griffith's pocket. "Let me tell you about your brother."

"Yes," said Griffith, handing Josiah the baseball again and inching forward in his seat.

"From the moment I laid eyes on that precious infant," Josiah said, "I knew the sign I had been waiting for had at long last arrived. My heart began to ache like it never had before." He teased the baseball's loose stitching with his fingernail. "No, not because I couldn't keep the child. Of course, I knew he had to be returned. But rather because of what else I was going to be parting with."

"The baseball," whispered Woody. "I reckon when you brought the boy back to his family, you gave it to Guy."

"That is correct, Mr. Woody," Josiah said. He reached across the table, returned the ball to Griffith, and then peered into the boy's eyes. "The moment I placed the baseball into your father's hand, I knew I had done right. My work was complete."

"I saw you that day," Griffith said softly.

"I know you did. I saw you, too."

"You didn't seem real." Griffith clutched the ball with both hands. "I'd never seen anyone who looked like you before. I ran off because I was scared."

"I remember." Josiah smiled. "You didn't hear what I said to your father when I handed him the baseball."

Griffith shook his head. He slipped the ball back into his pocket.

"I told your father the same things that Henry Chadwick had told me. I said it contained the key to all of baseball, the very future of the game. I said the baseball was intended for someone special, a young man who would carry the game into the twentieth century. I never said it was meant for your brother. I didn't want to make the same mistake twice. But there was no doubt in my mind that's who it was for." Josiah cleared his throat. "I simply told your father to keep his eyes and mind open. If he did, he would be able to see what others—what *I*—hadn't."

Griffith shuddered. "See the things that others don't," he said to Woody.

"When I returned your brother," Josiah went on, "my son chose not to accompany me on the journey. And upon arriving back at our cabin, I found him exactly where I had left him days earlier, sitting along the edge of the brook that ran through our orchard."

Josiah stood up. "From that day forth, every-thing changed."

Woody started to stand up too, but Josiah motioned for him to remain seated.

"We began to argue, my son and I," the old man continued. He headed for the door-way again. "We fought and fought like never before. And then one day, our war of words turned violent, physically violent. My son struck me, shoved me to the ground." Josiah paused. He still hadn't faced Griffith and Woody. "I did not hit back. My son was much bigger and stronger than I. He was already a robust man, twenty years of age. Yet even if he hadn't been, I would never have been able to strike my own child." Finally he turned. Tracks of tears ran along and through the creases below his eyes. "The next morning I woke up to an eerily quiet home. My son had left, and I knew he was never returning." Josiah shuffled back to the table. "Days later

I found his note. He'd left it in the orchard, right by the spot where he'd been sitting the day I returned from delivering baby Graham. His note contained just three words."

"Beware the Chancellor," Griffith said slowly, putting his hand on the baseball in his pocket.

Josiah's eyes widened. "You are correct, Mr. Griffith. 'Beware the Chancellor.' It was the first time I'd ever heard him refer to himself as such. In fact, it was several years before I learned that *he* was this Chancellor his note alluded to. However, to this day, I still do not know why he assumed the title."

"But how did you learn that—"

"The eagle," Griffith answered Woody's question before he even finished it.

"You are correct again, Mr. Griffith," said Josiah, frowning. "The eagle told me every last unimaginable horror that a father would never want to believe about his own offspring." He lowered his head and spoke to the table. "But I know it all to be true. I know the type of man my son has become." Josiah raised his eyes and stared at Griffith once again. "And now he must be stopped."

"That's why you're here," Griffith inserted.

"Indeed, Mr. Griffith. I would much prefer to spend my remaining days living a life of isolation and solitude, but that is not an option." Josiah swallowed. "I must once again walk among the world. For I know what he is capable of. I know what he wishes to accomplish."

"What does he want to do?" Woody asked.

Josiah pointed to Griffith's pocket. "If he gets his hand on that baseball, he will destroy the game as we know it. He desires to rule and control it." Josiah's frown deepened. "He wants to turn it into all that it was never meant to be."

"I reckon he's only one man," Woody said. "Granted, he has his thugs, but I don't see how one individual can wreak such havoc on so many. How's he goin' to control all of baseball?"

Griffith held his breath. Once again, he knew what Josiah's answer was going to be.

"Mr. Woody, Graham is the key to that control." Josiah nodded. "The Chancellor believes that Graham is the chosen one. If he were to gain possession of both the baseball and the boy, the Chancellor may very well rule the game and change it forever."

Woody squeezed the back of his neck. "Josiah, in your heart of hearts, do you believe he can be stopped?"

"Yes, I do," the old man answered without hesitation. "He must be. No matter the cost. Even if it means bringing great harm to my only offspring. The time has arrived for a father to take drastic measures."

"I reckon this is an awful lot to digest," Woody said, standing up. "If you don't mind, I'd like to excuse myself for a moment. I could use some fresh air, and I'm sure Dog wouldn't mind—"

"Mr. Woody," Josiah interrupted, motioning for him to sit back down, "I'm almost done. I'd prefer if you stayed a little while longer."

Woody looked over at Dog by the entranceway. Upon hearing his name, the hound had bounded to his feet. Despite his injured leg, Dog's hindquarters still shook with his rapidly wagging tail.

"A few more minutes," Woody said, returning to his seat. He gestured for Josiah to continue.

"Thank you. Indeed, there is one final thing we must discuss."

"You want to talk about the mole," said Griffith.

"Yet again, you are correct, Mr. Griffith," Josiah said, smiling. "That is information I did not learn from the eagle. I came to know it from the Chancellor's men themselves."

"They spoke to you?" Woody leaned in.

"I overheard them before the match in Nicollet Park," Josiah responded. "Some of the Chancellor's men can be quite careless with their tongues."

"But I reckon you don't know who this informant is?"

"No, that I do not."

"How do you know I'm not the mole?" asked Woody.

Josiah smiled. "Mr. Woody, when you look into a man's eyes—"

"Some things you just know," Griffith recited the words with Josiah.

Suddenly Dog scampered over to Woody and nestled up against his leg. Griffith looked down at Dog and smiled, but his smile quickly vanished. A strange feeling raced through his veins, a feeling of unease and fear. It reminded him of how he'd felt before the game a few days ago, when his mother had wanted Dog to stay with his sister, brother, and him.

Only the feeling Griffith had right now was much stronger.

He glanced across the table at Josiah. The elderly man was also focused on the hound, and from the way he was staring, Griffith was certain Josiah was feeling the same thing.

*Some things you just know.*

# 4

★

*Back on the Train Gang*

**oody held on** to the back of Griffith's shirt. "If your mother knew what we were about to do," he said, "she'd grab me by the—"

"Woody, we have to," Griffith cut him off.

"I reckon I don't feel comfortable puttin' your safety on the line like this."

Griffith crouched down as low as he could behind the rusty old rail cart with the over-grown weeds choking the wheels. "We don't have a choice," he whispered.

Under cover of the August night, Griffith, Woody, and Dog had snuck into the downtown rail yard. Griffith and Woody had scaled the tall wire fence and then dug a small hole for Dog to climb through. Once inside the yard, they'd discovered there was still another fence they'd need to clear. While the darkness had enabled them to maneuver without being detected, it also made moving around far more difficult. On the second fence, Woody caught his pants, tearing them and slicing a zigzagging gash that ran from his knee all the way to his ankle.

With the sun's early morning rays now illuminating the yard, the three needed to remain out of sight, for if they were spotted in the restricted area, they'd be arrested for trespassing in an instant. But that wasn't what was worrying Woody. At no point had the Rough Rider objected to the sneaking-in part of the plan. It was the part of the plan that came *next* that was causing his second thoughts.

"I reckon if anythin' were to happen to you, I would never be able to look your mother in the eye—"

"Nothing's going to happen!" Griffith cut him off again. "Josiah's come up with the perfect plan."

Shortly after midnight, Josiah had escorted Griffith, Woody, and Dog to the rail yard. Along the way, he'd explained to the three would-be stowaways how they would sneak aboard the train. Several times he reviewed the detailed, step-by-step instructions.

It was a far cry from how Woody had envisioned traveling to St. Louis. Originally he'd thought they would borrow ticket money from someone back at the university. Then, after meeting Josiah, he'd thought the old man would front them the necessary cash. However, Josiah didn't even have enough coin to cover his own costs. Because of his advanced age, he couldn't board a moving train, so he would need to purchase a ticket. For his travel expenses, he'd have to rely on his cunning and the willingness of strangers to assist an odd-looking, elderly man. He would travel separately and meet up with the barnstormers in New Orleans.

"You can't board in advance," he had reminded them as they prepared to scale the outer fence. "They inspect the boxcars for stowaways several times before departure. However, once those wheels are turning, you're in the clear."

Griffith glanced over his shoulder to Woody. "You ready?" he asked.

"I reckon let's you and I go over this one more time."

"Woody," Griffith said, shaking his head, "Josiah explained every last detail—"

"Amuse me, Griff," Woody interrupted.

Griffith sighed. "I've already jumped off a moving train," he said, lowering his hand into his pocket and gripping the baseball. "Hopping on can't be any more dangerous or difficult."

"I don't quite agree with you there. I wanna be sure you know what you're doin'." Woody's voice quivered. "As soon as that train starts to leave, you're runnin' like the wind for that open boxcar."

"Relax, Woody."

"You ain't stoppin' for anyone," Woody added. "Then, once I see you're safely onboard, I'll send Dog."

Griffith squeezed the baseball and glanced at Dog. The only part of the plan that concerned him was the one involving Dog. The scrappy hound's hind paw was still bothering him. He continued to hobble as he walked, and when he stood in one place, he raised the leg off the ground. Griffith felt the knot in the bottom of his stomach tighten, a knot he hadn't realized was there.

What if Dog couldn't make the leap?

"I reckon we're gettin' close," said Woody. He rolled his broad shoulders. "Be fixin' to fly, Griff."

Inching nearer to the end of the cart, Griffith gazed across the yard filled with empty freight cars, storage canisters, railroad posts, and signals. With his back foot, he dug in. . . .

*Chuff! Chuff!*

"Go!" Woody ordered.

Griffith was off before the first *chuff* finished chuffing. Leaping out from behind the rusty rail cart, he darted across the yard, dashing through puddles, hurdling tracks, and sidestepping cargo. In a matter of seconds, he was running alongside the accelerating train's massive steel wheels.

He reached across the rail into the open boxcar and inched closer to the train as he prepared to make his leap.

*Chuff! Chuff! Chuff!*

The train was gaining speed!

Running faster than he ever had, Griffith swung his arm across his body. He planted his hand on the floor of the boxcar and propelled himself onto the moving train. Rolling over and scrambling to his feet, he looked out toward Woody and Dog, who were racing for the train.

"Hurry!" Griffith shouted.

*Chuff! Chuff! Chuff! Chuff!*

Even though Woody and Dog were closing ground, the train was picking up more speed.

Griffith ran to the front of the boxcar, gripped the side of the open door, and leaned out. Gazing wide-eyed up the track, Griffith could see the rapidly approaching fence at the end of the rail yard. He gasped. What was beyond it? A body of water? A deep forest? A cliff?

"Hurry!" Griffith cried again.

"Get ready!" shouted Woody.

Griffith dove across the boxcar. Flat on his belly, he extended both hands and clapped for the canine.

Ordinarily Dog didn't wear a collar, but Josiah had fitted him with a temporary one for this very moment. Because the hound was injured, they weren't certain he'd be able to make the leap onto the train. The plan was to have Woody grab Dog by the collar and hoist him into the boxcar.

"Here he comes!" Woody called.

He reached down for the collar, but before he could slide his fingers around the leather strap, Dog dashed forward. Losing the limp, the hound burst past Woody and leaped for the train. Griffith leaned out as far as he could, wrapped his arms around Dog's lanky torso, and pulled him into the car.

Dog was aboard!

Suddenly Woody stumbled. He struggled to maintain his balance.

"Woody!" Griffith yelled.

The Rough Rider was somehow able to keep his feet, but he was no longer alongside the open boxcar.

*Chuff! Chuff! Chuff! Chuff! Chuff!*

"The fence!" Griffith screamed as the train reached the end of the yard. "Look out!"

Running full speed, Woody leaped into the air, spun his body a half turn, and squeezed through the narrow opening between the moving train and the metal fence. But he still wasn't onboard. Frantically waving his arms as he swatted aside branches and brush, he charged on.

Griffith glanced up the tracks. His jaw dropped at the sight of the bridge only a few hundred yards ahead. When the train reached the span, Woody wouldn't have any room left to run.

"C'mon!" Griffith urged as the Rough Rider

began to gain ground. "You can make it!"

For the second time, Griffith leaned out as far as he could.

"Come on, Woody!" he shouted, swiping for the Rough Rider.

"Almost there!" called Woody.

Suddenly the baseball rolled out of Griffith's pocket. Instinctively he reached with his other hand, grabbing hold of it inches from the boxcar's edge. He squeezed it harder than he ever had, and at the exact same instant, Woody lunged for Griffith's outstretched arm and latched on. Using all the strength he could muster—and some he didn't know he possessed—Griffith lifted Woody off the ground *with one hand* and flung the Rough Rider over his head into the boxcar . . . milli-moments before they reached the bridge.

The Rough Rider bounced to his feet, brushed off his clothes, and slid the boxcar door shut. "St. Louis, here we come!" he declared.

Woody lunged for Griffith's outstretched arm.

But for the moment, as Griffith lay flat back on his back and tried to regain his breath, all he could focus on was the baseball he held against his chest. There was no doubt in his mind that it had somehow helped him haul Woody into the car.

# 5

★

## Practice with the Superstars

**uby looked over at** her brother and grinned. As they walked along the riverside path leading to the practice field, the bounce in Graham's step and the smile on his face continued to grow. The ballists were enjoying the youngest Payne's anticipation too. Even Elizabeth, despite her reservations, couldn't help but be excited for her son.

She was allowing him to play. She'd made the decision only a short time ago, after the team had returned from distributing the fliers.

But now, heading toward the field, her team-mates were making sure she didn't change her mind.

"From your position behind the dish," the Professor noted, "you'll have Graham in your sights the entire time he's out in right garden."

"All stretching takes place alongside Graham Payne," declared Scribe.

"Since I'm not playing," Happy said, "I'll even keep a tally chart of how many times I check on him."

"See, Mom," Graham said, leaping in front of her. "You have nothing to worry about. Everyone's looking out for me."

Rounding a final bend, the practice field, located on a bluff overlooking the Mississippi River, came into full view. And what a field it was! Ruby couldn't imagine a more pictur-esque baseball setting. She gazed up into the cloudless Missouri sky. Even though it was

**DISH:**
*home plate.*

**RIGHT GARDEN:**
*right field. The outfield was once known as the garden. Left field was referred to as "left garden" and center field was called "center garden."*

a hot summer afternoon, the lack of humidity and gentle breeze off the water made it a beautiful one. Brilliant sunshine bathed the green oasis on which the local ballists were already warming up.

As the barnstormers approached the field, the players on the pitch gathered on the infield grass between home plate and the hill.

"Greetings," the Professor said. "We're the Travelin' Nine."

"We know who y'all are," the man who'd been pitching to his teammates said. "We've heard a lot about y'all in these parts."

Graham cupped his hand around his mouth. "Is that who I think it is?" he whispered in his sister's ear.

"It sure is," she replied.

"We're the St. Louis Superstars," said the hometown hurler. "I for one am looking forward to seeing how y'all do against the best there is."

**GREEN OASIS:** *playing field. Also called "pitch."*

**PITCH:** *playing field. Also called "green oasis."*

**HILL:** *pitcher's mound. Also called "bump" (see page 93).*

**HURLER:** *pitcher.*

Cy Young
Hurler

**ACE:**
*star pitcher.*

If anyone other than the tall, right-handed hurler had uttered such a statement, Ruby would have deemed him a braggart. But she knew better than to think that of Denton True Young, the finest and most durable pitcher the game of baseball had ever seen. Young was the ace of the Perfectos, the local professional team that was allowing their ballists to play for the amateur team, the Superstars, on their day off. Everyone in these parts (as well as everywhere the game of baseball was played) simply called him Cy because his fastball resembled a cyclone.

Ruby peeked over at Graham. With his arms folded across his chest, he stared wide-eyed at the ace. On the one hand, her brother appeared to be in awe, standing in the presence of such greatness. But at the same time, he seemed confident, as if he knew he'd be able to handle any pitch the hurler threw his way.

"We're short a player," Happy said. "We'd like for this young one over here to be our right scout." He motioned to Graham. "Would you be all right with that?"

Ruby held her breath. Even with her mother letting Graham play, she knew the final decision depended on the locals.

"We have plenty of ballists," said the lanky man standing behind Cy Young. "We'd gladly lend you one."

"That's very generous," the Professor said. "But we'd like the youngster to play. It's his birthday tomorrow, and—"

"Say no more," Cy Young interrupted. He

stepped forward and sized up Graham. "I'd love to take the hill against him."

"Thank you," said Elizabeth, using her man's voice.

Ruby flipped the hair off her neck. While the hometowners were amenable to Graham taking the field, she wondered how they would react if they found out that Guy was really Elizabeth.

"If that's the way y'all want it, that's the way it'll be," said Cy Young, stroking his chin. "But don't expect us to take it easy on him. That's not how we play the game 'round here."

**STRIKER:**
*batter, or hitter.*

With the Superstars standing on the sidelines, the Travelin' Nine took the field. Preacher Wil headed to the hill to throw batting practice to his teammates.

Out in right garden, Graham Payne stood on his toes and stared in at the striker,

84

determined to prove his worth on every single play.

The first ball that came his way was a sinking line drive just beyond the reach of Tales's glove. Charging, Graham caught the ball with his leather on the tips of the grass. He then quickly fired a one-hop throw to Bubbles, straddling second sack.

Graham's next chance wasn't even hit in his direction. It was an ant killer up the middle to Scribe in center garden. Graham scooted behind the supersize scout, just in case the ball got by him (which it didn't).

Graham fielded every batted ball hit in his direction. He made each catch seem more effortless than the next. And every one of his throws back to the infield hit the cutoff man on a fly or a single bounce.

"He's putting on a clinic," Ruby said to herself. Then she shouted, "Keep it up, Grammy!"

**LEATHER:** baseball glove or mitt.

**SACK:** base. Also called "bag" (see page 228).

**ANT KILLER:** ground ball. Also called "worm burner" (see page 309), "bug bruiser" (see page 351), "grass clipper" (see page 355), or "daisy cutter" (see page 381).

**CUTOFF MAN:** infielder who catches a throw from an outfielder in an attempt to hold up a base runner who is heading for a base or home plate or to get a ball to its intended target faster.

When Doc came to the plate for his cuts, Graham was finally tested. The Travelin' Nine's third sack man laced a stinger into the gap in right center. Slicing over in front of Scribe, Graham made a boot-string catch in full stride. He then skidded to a stop and fired a perfect pea into Tales.

**CUT:**
*swing.*

**THIRD SACK MAN:**
*third baseman. The first baseman was often called the "first sack man" and the second baseman was often called the "second sack man."*

"Just like Woody," Graham said to himself.

A couple of pitches later, Doc launched a sky ball destined for the trees beyond right garden. But at the crack of the lumber, Graham turned tail and somehow made an over-the-shoulder catch on a dead run inches from the woods. Bracing himself on one of the large trees, he whirled around and fired a one-hop throw to his cutoff man.

**STINGER:**
*hard-hit ball, usually a grounder or a line drive. Also known as "hammer" (see page 310).*

**BOOT-STRING CATCH:**
*running catch made near the ground.*

"Way to go!" Ruby cheered.

Graham raised his mitt and waved to his sister.

**PEA:**
*hard throw.*

From her perch atop the storage shed

in foul territory between the dish and third sack, Ruby waved back. After all Graham had been through over the last couple of days (and couple of months, for that matter), he deserved to enjoy his birthday weekend.

Still, Ruby wouldn't allow herself to let her guard down completely. For a moment her mind wandered back to earlier in the day.

"Everyone's passing out fliers," Professor Lance had announced at breakfast. "Everyone must see this magnificent city."

"Without a doubt," Happy had added. "I've visited St. Louis countless times and not once have I ever missed a chance to stroll her downtown streets. Nor will I ever."

Of course, there was another reason why the Professor and Happy had wanted the entire team to go. The Rough Riders knew Elizabeth wasn't about to let either Ruby or Graham advertise the match unless all the barnstormers accompanied them.

**SKY BALL:**
*fly ball to the outfield, or outer garden. Also sometimes referred to as "cloud hunter" (see page 89), "star chaser" (see page 95), or "skyscraper" (see page 392).*

**LUMBER:**
*baseball bat. Also called "timber" (see page 88) or "stick" (see page 335).*

**87**

They had a successful morning spreading the word about the footrace and the ball game (Happy had been able to coordinate *two* exciting events against the Superstars), but because Elizabeth was on edge, she had made the others nervous and antsy too. In front of the magnificent Old Courthouse, where the famous Dred Scott trial had taken place, a group of well-dressed lawyers hustled past. Tales had been so startled by the sight of men in suits he accidentally dropped his fliers. Ruby even saw Scribe jump a couple of times.

"Last one," Preacher Wil declared.

The sound of the hurler's voice brought Ruby back from her daydream. She looked toward the hill where the southpaw was showing the rock to Bubbles, standing at the line.

"Put it right here," said Bubbles, pointing his lumber to where he wanted the pitch

**SOUTHPAW:**
*left-handed individual; the commonly used nickname for players who throw left-handed.*

**ROCK:**
*baseball. Also called "pill" or "rawhide."*

**THE LINE:**
*the batter's box.*

**PILL:**
*baseball. Also called "rock" or "rawhide."*

**TIMBER:**
*baseball bat. Also called "lumber" (see page 87) or "stick" (see page 335).*

**RAWHIDE:**
*baseball. Also called "pill" or "rock."*

to cross the plate. "I want to make Graham run."

Preacher Wil tipped his cap, rocked into his delivery, and put the pill exactly where Bubbles had requested.

*Crack!*

The moment the ball struck timber, Graham gave chase. With both eyes fixed on the rawhide, he darted after the tailing cloud hunter. Sprinting toward the foul line, he lunged for the ball. In full flight, he made the spectacular catch. But that was just the beginning. Graham tumbled to the ground, somersaulted twice, and sprang to his feet. He then lifted the pill from his leather and raised it up high, showing everyone he'd completed the sensational snag.

Since Graham was the next and final visiting ballist to take batting practice, he turned around and jogged in backward, just like Woody always did.

**CLOUD HUNTER:** *fly ball to the outfield, or outer garden. Also sometimes referred to as "sky ball" (see page 87), "star chaser" (see page 95), or "skyscraper" (see page 392).*

**FOUL LINES:** *lines extending from home plate through first and third base and all the way to the outfield. Anything within the lines is considered to be in fair territory; anything outside the lines is in foul territory.*

89

Just like Woody . . .

"He doesn't need the baseball here to make magical plays," Happy said to Ruby. He shielded the sun from his eyes as he peered up at her on top of the storage shed.

"No, he doesn't," replied Ruby. Sliding down the slanted roof, she landed next to the old-timer, who'd just walked over. "But I'd still like to get it back."

Ruby dropped her hand into her empty pocket and sighed. At least she no longer had to concern herself with keeping the baseball a secret. After the attack, she'd come clean about the ball, even telling the team how she and her brothers had been using it. They had known about it all along.

"You'll get that baseball back," Happy said confidently. "I'm not worried in the least. Woody and Griffith will bring it here."

"Woody, Griffith, and Dog," Ruby corrected.

She glanced out at Preacher Wil on the

hill. He seemed a little lost without his dog, but baseball was a welcome distraction. It was for her as well. For a few minutes she wasn't worrying as much about Griffith. She wasn't wondering if he, Woody, and Dog had found shelter. She wasn't scared they'd encountered the Chancellor's thugs. She could . . .

"Don't worry, Ruby," said Graham, jogging up. He slipped between his sister and Happy. "Griff's fine. He'll be back with us before you know it."

"I'm not worried," Ruby said, making a face. "What makes you think I am?"

Graham chuckled. "Whether you realize it or not, you're a lot like Griff. Especially when he's not here." Graham flipped his hair and then imitated his sister's voice. "You might think you're able to hide what's going on inside your head, but I can see in like I'm looking through a window."

"Excuse me," Cy Young said, walking in

their direction. "If y'all don't mind, I'd like to pitch to the lad."

Graham clapped his hands. "Absolutely!"

Cy Young turned to Preacher Wil still standing on the bump. "Is it okay with you?"

Preacher Wil flipped the ball to the ace. "Absolutely!" he replied. He winked at Graham. "Show him what you can do."

Graham glanced to his sister. "I'm getting to hit against Cy Young! What a birthday present!"

**BUMP:**
*pitcher's mound. Also called "hill" (see page 81).*

"You play a mighty fine right garden," said Cy Young, resting his leather on Graham's shoulder. "But around here, between those white lines, I'm in charge." He headed for the hill.

"If you say so," Graham said. He picked up a bat, pointed to the field, and looked at Ruby again. "It's time for Graham the Great to take his swings."

"Graham the Great?" Ruby eyed him sideways. "I'm so glad you're not letting playing for the Travelin' Nine go to your head."

"I'm simply going to demonstrate my superior skills," Graham said, inflating his chest and beaming. "I guess there's a good side to Griffith and Woody not being here."

"They'll be back before you know it," said Ruby, mocking Graham's words from moments ago. She laughed. "They're going to get here seconds before the first pitch."

Graham stopped smiling. "Don't I know it," he grumbled.

"And the second they get here, you come out!"

"But right now," Graham said, wagging his timber at Cy Young, "I'm going to battle the best hurler there is!"

As Graham headed to the line, he began to wonder whether it had been such a good idea to boast the way he had. Griffith wouldn't have liked to hear him talk in such a manner, and his father would never have approved. While he'd been bragging, his mother hadn't said a word; her silence spoke, though.

Setting himself at the plate, Graham peered out at Cy Young. The ace hurler shook his head and smirked; he wasn't about to let some little kid show him up. Even though this was batting practice and the hurler was *supposed* to groove pitches over the plate, Graham knew his mouth had changed the rules. Cy Young would be gunning for him, overpowering him with his trademark heater.

"C'mon, Grams," he whispered to himself. "You can do this."

He shut his eyes and took a long breath. He was going to time Cy Young's windup, start his swing early, and then launch a star chaser toward the Mississippi.

From behind him along the third base line, Tales began delivering the play-by-play: "Now here's Graham Payne, baseball's new wonder boy. This sultan of swat may stand four feet nothing, but when he connects with

**HEATER:** *fastball.*

**STAR CHASER:** *fly ball to the outfield, or outer garden. Also sometimes referred to as "sky ball" (see page 87), "cloud hunter" (see page 89), or "skyscraper" (see page 392).*

the timber, he can launch a ball a country mile. He steps in against the lanky right-hander whose nickname comes from a force of nature. Who will win this epic confrontation? Who will win this classic duel? The little prodigy stares down the hurler. Cy Young rocks into his windup. Around comes his arm, and here's the pitch. Graham swings. . . ."

*Whiff!*

"A mighty swing and a miss by the lad!" Tales announced. "Strike one! Oh, was he ever overmatched on that pitch. Now the one-of-a-kind hurler stares back at the youngster, who's pounding the plate. You can tell the little prodigy is itching for a second chance. Here it comes. . . ."

*Whiff!*

"Strike two!" called Tales. "And on that one young Graham Payne corkscrews himself right into the ground. You can see the frustration all over the boy wonder's face. He doesn't know what to do at the dish. If this were a prizefight, the referee would step in. But since there is no referee, Cy Young is rocking into his windup once again. He lets fly. Graham swings. . . ."

*Whiff!*

"Swung on and missed!" Tales declared. "Strike three! Dessert has been served. A heaping portion of humble pie for Graham Payne!"

# Saturday Sports Spectacular

## AUGUST 26, 1899

### Twice the Excitement! Twice the Entertainment!

COME WATCH THE GREATEST HURLER
EVER TO TAKE THE HILL....

## Denton True "Cy" Young

WITNESS WITH YOUR OWN
EYES THE LEGENDARY

COUNT THE STRIKEOUTS
HOW MANY WILL HE TOTAL?

CYCLONE FASTBALL

10? 15? 27?

# Footrace

SPRINT ACROSS THE MISSISSIPPI RIVER

TIME: 8:00 A.M. • LOCATION: ST. LOUIS BRIDGE • **Admission: 5 cents**

# BASEBALL MATCH

# ST. LOUIS SUPERSTARS

## VS.

# THE TRAVELIN' NINE

Game Time: 1:00 p.m.    Location: South 1st Street Field

Admission: **25 cents**

# 6

★

## San Antonio

**ith Dog's head**
resting in his lap,
Griffith sat cross-
legged on the floor of
the empty boxcar. He
stared intently at Woody, sitting across from
him and leaning against the far wall. Even
though the doors were closed, the inside of
the car was well lit. Slivers of daylight filtered through the sides, lining the floor like
tiger stripes, and the pumpkin-shaped hole
in the roof served as a natural chandelier.

Safely aboard the moving freight train bound for St. Louis, Woody, Griffith, and Dog had wanted to sleep, but the three stowaways were much too charged up for rest. So Woody had started to talk. He began to tell his traveling companions all about the Rough Riders, starting with their training days in San Antonio, Texas.

"'In whose veins the blood stirred with the same impulse which once sent the Vikings over sea,'" Woody said. "Those were the words of Colonel Roosevelt. He expected his recruits to be men of action, and were we ever."

"He brought you to San Antonio?" asked Griffith.

Woody shook his head. "We were there before him," he replied. "Best I recall, the colonel got there on the fifteenth or sixteenth of May, and I reckon what he found on his arrival was the most undisciplined group of volunteers in military history. Sure we were all skilled with pistols and rifles, and each one of us could ride a horse better than the next, but we needed to be trained." Woody pointed at Griffith. "The best military man a young soldier could ever ask for trained us. He didn't treat us like volunteers. He treated us like regulars. He paid no mind to the color of our skin, the size of our bank accounts, or where a man was from." He motioned for the baseball in Griffith's pocket. "Because like Colonel Roosevelt told us, when it came time for battle, a bullet wasn't gonna know the diff'rence between a member of the First Volunteer Cavalry and a regular."

Griffith rolled the baseball across the boxcar floor to Woody. The Rough Rider picked up the sphere and held it in the palm of his open hand. For several moments he examined the object, looking at it from different angles and from time to time rotating it ever so slightly with the index finger of his other hand.

Then, for the better part of the next hour, Woody talked about what life was like for the soldiers in San Antonio. He spoke of the endless hours of training, how Colonel Roosevelt made them master the basic drills on foot *and* horseback. He talked about how brutally exhausted they were each and every night, but despite the fatigue and heat and wind and dust and mosquitoes the size of moths, they all managed to get up the next morning and train harder than the previous day.

Sometimes the Rough Rider's words were identical to ones that Griffith remembered. He'd shut his eyes, and for a few fleeting seconds, he'd be able to hear his father's voice all over again. At other times Woody's recollections were nothing like Guy's. Griffith found it fascinating to listen to the exact same tales told from a new and different point of view.

Then Woody started talking about Guy.

"Your pop created a family among us soldiers. He built this mighty and unbreakable trust. Not only through his actions and deeds, but also through his words. I can't even begin to tell you how many stories we heard about you and Ruby and Grammy, and of course, dear Elizabeth. I reckon some of us felt we came to know the members of your family better than we knew some of our own!" Woody laughed. "Your pop shaped the nine of us—Owen, Professor Lance, Crazy Feet, Scribe, Happy, Tales, Bubbles, himself, and me—into a team of brothers. Even gave us our names." He laughed again and shook his head. "I lived in Pittsburgh and spent years in a *steel* factory—so he nicknamed me Woody. Go figure." Woody paused. He picked up the baseball, which had been resting on his knee, and held it out to Griffith. "I reckon this here was our foundation. This was our rock."

Griffith lifted Dog's head from his lap. He stood up, walked across the boxcar, and sat down shoulder-to-shoulder with the Rough Rider.

Putting the baseball on Griffith's leg, Woody began speaking of the night the order was issued that they were finally heading for Cuba. At first the volunteers had been elated, but their excitement had quickly dissipated when they learned that the horses on which they'd trained wouldn't be allowed to go. There simply wasn't enough room. Then came word that there wasn't enough room for many of the soldiers to go either.

"But all of you went," Griffith noted.

"All nine of us," Woody said, nodding. "Against *impossible* odds. You ask any mathematician. Impossible odds. I reckon every which way we turned, there were grown men cryin' like babies, devastated that they hadn't been selected to serve their country. But the nine volunteers who . . ." Woody stopped. He reached over and placed the baseball back into Griffith's hand, closed his fingers around it, and squeezed them gently. "It was because of this, Griff. No doubt in my mind. No doubt in any of our minds."

Woody then spoke about the journey from San Antonio to Tampa, where many of the soldiers were stationed before being deployed to Cuba. "We spent a week in Tampa," Woody continued. "Must've been twenty-five thousand of us there, all preparin' for war. But there was no order or system. I reckon it was pretty much every man for himself. Heck, it was such a muddled mess that some among us began to wonder if we'd ever make the trip to Cuba." Woody sighed. "What a voyage that turned out to be."

The journey across the waters in the *Yucatan* was a brutal ordeal. The soldiers baked under the tropical sun; they didn't have any fresh meat or vegetables; and the little water they had was filthy and rancid. But even under these harsh conditions, Colonel Roosevelt forced the men to prepare for battle. For hours at a time, the soldiers studied strategies and practiced tactics.

"On the mornin' of June twenty-second," Woody went on, "we were awoken at three thirty. We were goin' ashore. Our destination was Daiquirí, Cuba." He took the baseball from Griffith again. "I reckon those transport boats tossed us about like rag dolls. I don't think there was a single one of us who didn't get seasick. All day long, we helped one another scramble onto the beach and struggle to set up camp. By nightfall, thousands and thousands of American soldiers were safely on land." Woody's face turned grim as he held the baseball to his chest. "Griff, we suffered only a couple casualties that day, but I reckon it was chaos on that beach. Heck, it made the situation back in Tampa seem downright orderly. Bombs burstin' and buildings burnin' everywhere you looked. And nightfall brought little relief. Not only did we fear ambush, we also had to contend with the heaviest and steadiest rains any of us had ever seen. And I won't even get into those eerie land-crab creatures."

Griffith stood back up and headed over to the corner of the boxcar. Through a crevice above the door hinge, he gazed out at the passing countryside.

"I still don't understand something about San Antonio," he said, speaking to the scenery. "The fact that all nine of you got chosen for Cuba defied the laws of probability. I get that. But I keep thinking there had to have been something more." He turned to Woody.

"I'm sure of it. There had to have been something else that convinced the Rough Riders there was something *magical* about the baseball."

"There most certainly was something else, Griff," Woody said, smiling. "I was saving it for when I talked about San Juan Hill, but I'll share it with you now instead."

Griffith gazed at the Rough Rider, who had a faraway look in his eyes. He then sat down beside Dog, who rested his snoot back on Griffith's leg.

"It took place at the Menger Hotel," Woody began, holding the baseball to his chest again. "We were all in the lounge, like we so often were after a gruelin' day of training. But that evening Colonel Roosevelt was there with us, first time he ever was. Like always, your pop was spinnin' tales, talking about home life and family. He started tellin' us 'bout young Graham, how one day out on the green oasis he smacked the pill—"

"I always thought Roosevelt didn't like baseball," Griffith interrupted.

"Didn't like?" Woody replied. "Heck, he hated it! Didn't even consider it a sport. Called it a leisure activity." He chuckled. "But your pop was a brave soul. He just kept on talkin' 'bout Graham and baseball. As a matter of fact, he was holdin' *the* baseball the entire time, rubbin' it and massaging it like he so often did." He wagged a finger at Griffith. "But after a while, Colonel Roosevelt started scoffing at all the baseball talk, sayin' how the only real sports were hunting and horses." Woody shook his head. "You know what he did? He ripped the baseball right out of your pop's hands. I kid you not. This here baseball." Woody held up it. "You don't need me to tell you that's something *no one* should do. Not even Colonel Roosevelt."

"What did my dad do?"

Woody chuckled. "I reckon he couldn't pull rank on the colonel. So he decided to wait and see how things played out." He tossed the ball to Griffith. "The colonel walked to the far side of the lounge and set the baseball down on top of a bottle. Then he headed back to your pop and drew his revolver."

Griffith gasped. "In the middle of the lounge?"

"Sure did," Woody replied, nodding. "He pointed it 'cross that crowded room. Then he glanced over at your pop and said, 'This is what I think of baseball.'" Woody cleared his throat. "Griff, Colonel Roosevelt is a great shot, one of the best shots I've ever seen. He fired every last bullet in that revolver, unloaded the entire chamber. And even though I was duckin' for cover like everyone else, I watched that baseball hop, skip, and jump with my own two eyes. We all did." Woody patted his chest. "Colonel Roosevelt

"This is what I think of baseball."

knew it wasn't in his best interest to stick around after shootin' off his weapon in a crowded lounge. He was out the door before any of us even had the chance to sit back down on our stools. As soon as he left, your pop was first to his feet. You know what he found?"

Griffith shook his head.

"At the time, neither did we. Your pop was so upset, he just picked his baseball off the floor, stuffed it into his pocket, and headed straight for the exit. We didn't see him again till we got back to camp. He was sittin' alone by the fire, talkin' to himself. Talkin' 'bout Graham, just like he had been when Colonel Roosevelt had snatched his prized possession from his hands." Woody began to smile. "Griff, your pop had the most amazed looked on his face, and I reckon once we stood next to him, we all saw why. He was holding his baseball. And it didn't have a single bullet hole in it. Not a mark or scratch on it either."

Griffith looked down at the baseball he held in his cupped hands. "How could that be?" he asked.

Woody shrugged. "I reckon that was nothing compared to what happened in Cuba."

# 7

★

## The War in Cuba

he crocodile," Woody said.

"A crocodile?" Griffith looked at him oddly. "What about a crocodile?"

"Whenever I talk about the war in Cuba," Woody replied, "I always start with the crocodile. I know that must sound strange, but I reckon you'll understand why I do in a moment." He rested his hands on his bowlegs. "A coupla mornings after comin' ashore, we headed out on our first mission into the jungle. The jungle's a terrifyin' place, Griff, 'specially to soldiers who ain't never seen one before. It's a wet world with no sky, and when you're walkin' through for that first time, you can't help but wonder if you'll ever again see the blue above or feel a fresh breeze on your skin. I reckon not a single one of us dared to stray more than a few yards from the next."

"Where was Colonel Roosevelt?"

"Leadin' the way like he always was. We found comfort in knowin' that our commanding officer, the man who'd issued the marching orders, was out front."

"Where was my dad?" Griffith leaned in. "Where was the baseball?"

"Prior to settin' out into the jungle, it was in your pop's hand. Right along with his weapon, believe it or not." Woody reached over and took the baseball from Griffith's lap. "But then when we headed off, he did something with this here ball he ain't never done before." Woody held up a finger. "I'll get to that shortly."

Griffith lifted his hands, which had been resting on Dog's back, and pretended to hold a rifle. He couldn't fathom how his father would've been able to hold his weapon and the baseball at the same time.

"I reckon our terror grew with each step we took," Woody continued. "We knew the enemy used smokeless cartridges, and that meant once them shots started ringin' out, we wouldn't be able to tell if they was shootin' from down low or behind. We were deathly afraid of guerrilla attacks comin' at us from the edges of the jungle and from the trees above."

"Gorillas?" Griffith's eyes widened. "There were gorillas in Cuba?"

"Not that kind of gorilla!" Woody laughed. "Guerrillas. Warriors who sneak up on you, who don't abide by the rules of warfare."

He shook his head. "But before we encountered guerrillas, we came face-to-face with that Cuban crocodile, and yes, Griff, it was a real crocodile. Out of nowhere he scuttled into our path, separating us from our commanding officer. I reckon none of us had ever seen such a creature, and those menacing, snapping jaws frightened us like nothing before."

"Did someone shoot it?"

Woody wagged a finger at Griffith. "If that Cuban croc had wanted to, he could've devoured two or three of us before any of us could've raised a weapon. If he wanted to. But he didn't, Griff. Nor did we want to harm it. And you know why? Because he wasn't the enemy. The only reason he had anything to do with *our* war was because we happened to be fightin' it in *his* home."

"So what did you do? How did you get around it?"

Woody paused. "We did what the crocodile *told* us to do."

"How did the crocodile tell you what to
do?" Griffith asked, stroking Dog gently
above the ridges over his eyes.

"By pointin' his snout," Woody replied.
"Told us to take a different route, a slight
detour. So we did.

"As soon as we started down that other
route, the grenades began to explode, and
the bullets began to fly. We ducked for cover,
and with our bellies pinned to the earth, all
any of us could do was listen helplessly to the
cries of the wounded. That skirmish seemed
to last for hours, but in reality, it was over in
mere minutes."

"Did any of you get hit?"

"Not a single one of us," Woody answered,
shaking his head. "One more thing that
defied the odds." He wagged his finger
again. "The path that crocodile wouldn't

let us take? Nothin' left of it. Turned into a giant hole in the ground. I reckon if not for that creature tellin' us which way to go, we all would've been blown to pieces." Woody paused. "That crocodile knew it too, because when the smoke cleared, he was right there beside that hole. Almost as if he was checkin' to make sure we'd survived. And if you ask me—or any of the Rough Riders—I'm certain he winked and nodded our way before disappearin' into the jungle."

"Like the horses back in Louisville," Griffith whispered.

Woody nodded. "I reckon when we saw them thoroughbreds in the River City and that gigantic cow in Chicago, each and every one of us thought back to that Cuban croc. That's why we weren't afraid, Griff. Whenever we see animals or birds or whatever appearin' or actin' out of the ordinary, we know it's for our own good. The crocodile taught us that." He flipped the ball to Griffith. "But that was nothing."

"Nothing?"

"Nothing compared to the most incredible—impossible—thing any of us ever experienced: San Juan Hill."

Griffith slid his legs out from under Dog's head, stood up, and walked back to the corner of the boxcar. Peering through the crevice above the door hinge, he gazed out at the rolling hills and prairies. Suddenly he realized that unlike previous train rides, this one hadn't made him queasy. It must be because he'd been far too riveted by every last word out of Woody's mouth.

He turned back toward the Rough Rider and leaned against the wall, bending one leg so that the bottom of his boot was pressed flat against the side of the boxcar. Then he raised the baseball to his chest and nodded to Woody.

For the first time in his life, Griffith Payne was ready to hear about what really happened on San Juan Hill.

"We waited for the order to begin our charge in a storm of shells and rifle fire," Woody said. "We were sittin' ducks, crouchin' and hidin' behind anything we could find and unable to move from our position 'cause there was no artillery to provide us cover." He rubbed his temples. "Griff, San Juan Hill was the first time we ever saw fear in your pop's face. Soldiers were droppin' all round us, and I for one started to cry. I admit it. Tears flowed from my eyes. Tears of terror."

Griffith felt *his* eyes beginning to swell. He started back over to Woody.

"Finally the order arrived. We began the surge. Led by Colonel Roosevelt, 'course." Woody spoke in bursts, struggling to form complete thoughts. "Your pop was first to follow. Then we all did. Charged up that hill.

*Sluggers*

Till we reached a clearing. Some thought we'd made it all the way to the summit. Heck, I can still see the disappointment on their faces when they learned we'd only made it a few feet. Up a first chain of hills. We still had a ways to go."

Griffith sat down next to Woody, and as soon as he did, Dog settled in beside him. Like before, the hound laid his head on Griffith's leg.

"'We're taking the Heights!' Roosevelt suddenly shouted. 'These hills belong to the Rough Riders.' Under even heavier fire, we plowed forward. Your pop was hot on the colonel's heels, echoing his rallyin' cries." Woody reached across and took the baseball from Griffith again. "That's when it happened. Your Uncle Owen was right beside me, as close as you are to me, when that bullet struck his leg. *Thump!*"

Griffith winced.

"For as long as I breathe, I reckon I'll

124

never forget the sound of bullet meetin' flesh." Woody grimaced as he spoke. "Your uncle Owen crumpled to the ground. Scribe, Crazy Feet, and I found cover underneath some brush, not too far from the others. We thought Owen would be able to crawl to us. But he couldn't move. Only scream. Heck, to this day I can still hear his wails in my head." Woody wrapped his hands tightly around the baseball. "After what seemed like an eternity, but surely was only several seconds, Owen began to move. Ever so slowly. Rose to his knees." He looked away. "That's when the second bullet caught him."

"Uncle Owen was shot twice?" Griffith gasped. "I thought he only—"

"Hold on." Woody turned back. A single tear was sliding down his left cheek. He placed his hand on Griffith's leg and gently squeezed. "Let me tell the whole tale, Griff. That second shot hit him right here." Woody patted his chest with the ball. "He

125

went down faster than the first time." His jaw tightened. Beads of sweat formed on his temples. "At that point, your pop bolted for his brother, but before he could take two steps, Scribe had him by the arm. He struggled mightily to break free, so Bubbles and Crazy Feet grabbed hold as well. They couldn't let him go out there. Not even for his own siblin'." Woody began to nod. "So

Doc did. From out of nowhere, Doc charged
over to your uncle Owen."

"Doc?" Griffith made a confused face.
"When did he get there?"

"None of us had ever seen him before,"
Woody said, smiling. "I reckon he wasn't in
our company. But there he was, steppin' into
the line of fire. Stranger helpin' stranger."

"So Doc brought Uncle Owen to safety."

Woody squeezed Griffith's leg again. "As soon as Doc reached Owen, he placed his hands on his chest, right where that bullet had pierced his uniform. Now keep in mind, Griff, this whole time your pop was still tryin' to break free of his fellow Rough Riders. He was yellin' at the top of his lungs. Urgin' his brother to hang on just a little while longer. Callin' out the names of all the people who mattered most to him. When he said your brother Graham's name . . ." Woody stopped.

"What happened? Tell me."

Woody placed the ball in Griffith's lap. "I can't tell you what happened," he said. "I can only tell you what I'm *told* happened."

"I don't understand." Griffith tilted his head. "What do you mean?"

"Griff, the next thing I saw—the next thing *we* saw—was your uncle Owen lyin' on the ground right beside us. Your pop was hovering over him. The two brothers were clutchin' the baseball.'"

"How did Uncle Owen get there?"

Woody shrugged. "I can tell you what your pop told me. He only spoke of it one time."

"He didn't tell anyone else? Just you?"

"Later that evening," Woody replied, nodding. He spoke in bursts again. "'Course, I shared what he told me with my fellow Rough Riders. That's how your pop wanted it. Asked me to be his liaison. So he'd never have to talk about the horror again. The rest of us discussed it. Many times. But we never could make sense of it. All we can say for certain is that somethin' inexplicable— somethin' beyond words—took place during the insanity on San Juan Hill." Woody let out a long breath. "Griff, for a few moments on that battlefield, time stood still. For all of us. But not for your pop."

"That's what my dad told you?"

"In vivid detail," Woody said. "I reckon there are a couple things 'bout that conversation that always come to mind." He held up two fingers. "First, your pop *needed* to tell someone 'bout what he experienced. If he didn't, it couldn't possibly be true. But I still don't know why he chose to tell me."

Griffith held tight to the baseball. "What's the second thing?" he asked.

"Your pop believed he could have done more."

"More?"

Woody sat up tall. "When your pop called out your brother's name, everything on that battlefield came to a halt. And I do mean everything. Bullets and birds stopped flyin'. In the heat of that midsummer cauldron, everything *froze* in midair." He nodded. "Guy Payne was the only one with the ability to maneuver through the still. He raced out to your uncle Owen and lifted Doc's hand from his chest. That's when your pop discovered the wound wasn't a fatal one. 'Cause Owen was holdin' the baseball."

"Wait." Griffith held up a hand. "How did Uncle Owen get the baseball?"

Woody nodded and smiled. "Remember when I told you earlier how right before we headed out into the jungle your pop did something with this here baseball that he hadn't ever done before?"

"He let Uncle Owen hold the baseball," Griffith whispered.

"He sure did," said Woody, the faraway gaze returning to his eyes. "He gave the baseball to his brother. I reckon we all saw the gesture. It registered with each and every one of us, 'cause it was the first and only time your pop ever *willingly* gave up possession of that baseball. Griff, it was almost as if he knew your Uncle Owen *needed* to hold on to it."

Cradling the baseball in his palm, Griffith

raised it to eye level. Then he spun his wrist a quarter turn and peered into the hole.

"That baseball saved your uncle Owen's life," Woody said. "I reckon that bullet in there was meant for his heart. You ask any of the Rough Riders. That is something we all believe."

Griffith stood back up and walked to the center of the boxcar. He held the baseball to the sunlight coming through the pumpkin-shaped hole in the ceiling.

"But Uncle Owen lost his leg," he said while studying the ball. "Why couldn't the baseball prevent that?"

"I reckon the Rough Riders have wrestled with that question as well," Woody answered. "That baseball wasn't there to protect a limb. It was there to preserve a life. And that it did. Life over limb."

"Tell me the rest," said Griffith, lowering the ball and turning back to Woody. "You said my father thought he could've done more. What did you mean?"

"After determining that Owen wasn't fatally wounded, your pop carried him to safety. Placed him down alongside myself and the others. He went back for Doc and moved him out of harm's way too. Then he decided to head out into the open battle-field for a *third* time. He went to move the bullets."

Griffith's eyes widened. "What do you mean *move*?"

"I reckon this is that 'more' part, Griff," Woody replied. "Your pop had no idea when time would start up again. He didn't know if he had seconds or minutes. Nor did he know what was going to trigger it. For all he knew, his touchin' a bullet would restart everything, and he'd be caught in the line of fire. However, he risked it anyway. But after shiftin' less than a handful of bullets, he realized there were simply far too many. He was goin' to have to choose which ones to move. So he started movin' the ones he thought were aimed at the Rough Riders." Woody held out his hands. "Now if you ask me, I don't see how he could possibly have been able to tell. But your pop claims he could. Says he redirected one headin' right for Bubbles's temple."

"The one that hit his ear?"

Woody nodded. "I believe so. But it upset your father that it hit him at all. Same with the bullet intended for Professor Lance. That one clipped and shattered his spectacles."

"His eye patch."

"His eye patch," Woody echoed. "But like I said, I don't see how your pop could've been able to tell which bullets were headin' where. I tried tellin' him that. Told him the bullets that hit Bubbles and the Professor could've just as easily been two that had been farther away. And by movin' the bullets he did, he actually saved their lives. But your pop wasn't hearin' it."

"How did time start up again?"

"The very same way it stopped. Your pop was beggin' your uncle Owen to hang on. Holdin' his hand and tellin' him all the wonderful things he had to live for. I reckon when he said Graham's name, the world unfroze. And like I already told you, the next thing we saw was Owen lyin' on the ground right beside us, with your pop hoverin' over him. Doc was right next to the wounded soldier."

"That's why you started calling him Doc," Griffith guessed.

"What else were we gonna call him?" Woody let out a short laugh. "Though Doc was no more a medic than any of us. Still, he went right to work as if he was a doctor. Your uncle Owen was losin' blood fast, and it was Doc who tied that tourniquet round his leg. Doc wanted to save that limb, but on the battlefield . . ." Woody's voice trailed off.

"Life over limb," Griffith whispered.

"Life over limb," Woody repeated. He pinched the bridge of his nose. "Griff, more than two hundred men lost their lives that day. Over a thousand more were wounded. But all of us survived." He reached for the ball. "I reckon we have your father and this here baseball to thank for that. It changed lives. It saved lives."

# 8

★

## Truman

**riffith pressed his** palms to his temples and pulled on his thick hair. At the moment, the only things traveling faster than the freight train were the worrisome thoughts bombarding his brain. He'd attempted to focus on pleasant memories—playing catch with Graham in the yard, the family trip to Boston two summers ago, planting tomatoes and cucumbers in the garden with Mom— but his fears kept taking over.

Inside the dimly lit boxcar, he tried befriending the repetitive sounds—the rumbling and grinding of the steel wheels, the clicking of the passing railroad ties, the rattling of the metal lock against the open door, and Woody's snoring.

Exhausted from sharing his war stories, the Rough Rider had fallen asleep seconds after finishing his last sentence. At the time, the light of day still hadn't faded, so Griffith had watched his traveling companion sleep. Woody had pulled his cap down over his face, and his brim would rise and fall with each snore.

Griffith squeezed the back of his neck. At long last, he knew what had happened in Cuba. More than ever, he was in awe of the Rough Riders, amazed by their valor. He was proud to know each and every one of them and—

*Who is the mole? Who is the turncoat?*

One of the soldiers was no longer on their side. He couldn't think it. He couldn't stop thinking it.

Griffith glanced down at Dog, resting his snoot on his leg like he so often did. He stroked the back of the hound's neck and ran his fingers along the animal's muscled torso. He was counting on Dog and his keen judgment of character. When they arrived in St. Louis, his canine friend would help him figure out which one of the Travelin' Nine was a traitor.

Griffith closed his eyes and shook his head.

How could one of their own betray them? How could one of these American heroes align himself with the Chancellor? The Rough Riders were men of honor, good men, true men.

"True men," he whispered to himself. "A true man doesn't—"

"You have a name."

Suddenly Dog's ears perked up. He lifted his head, sat up tall, and then stared back at Griffith with a look in his eyes that the boy had never seen before.

"Truman?"

Griffith sighed. He thought about the way he often spotted Preacher Wil gazing at Dog, and for the first time, he saw what Preacher Wil must have. There was a nobility to Dog. The hound loved unconditionally. Faithful and trustworthy, Dog possessed the qualities that Preacher Wil hoped to find in himself and others, the traits that true men should aspire to have.

Dog smiled. He didn't *appear* to smile or *seem* to smile. Dog *smiled* at Griffith.

"Truman," Griffith repeated. "You have a name." He reached out and shook the hound's paw. "Truman."

# 9

★

## *The Sprint Across the River*

**hielding her eyes** from the brilliant early morning sunshine, Ruby could hardly believe what she saw: a line of people that snaked almost an entire city block, waiting to pay their five cents admission so that they could stand on the St. Louis Bridge to witness the Sprint Across the River.

Ruby stood by herself a few yards beyond the tables by the entrance, where the ballists from both squads were collecting money and passing out tickets. Stepping closer to the railing, she carefully peeked over the edge. Beneath the three-spanned steel arch bridge, the mighty Mississippi glistened as the morning rays reached the waters.

"Start this day off right, Crazy Feet," she whispered to the river below.

"You talking to yourself again?"

Ruby turned. She was surprised to see Graham standing inches away. She hadn't heard him walk up.

"If it wasn't your birthday," she said, shaking her fist, "I would—"

"I don't know, Ruby," Graham cut her off. He stood on his toes and compared his height to hers with a hand. "Now that I'm eight, I'm almost as tall as you. One day real soon, I will be." He flexed his eyebrows. "And I'll be stronger than you too."

"One day," she replied, playfully shoving him away, "but not yet."

"It's my birthday!" Graham continued. "Great things are going to happen. Just you watch." He waved to the crowd. "Look at how many people are here. If Crazy Feet wins this dash, we'll earn a hundred dollars! More!"

Graham was right. So long as Crazy Feet won the winner-take-all footrace (being held to determine which team would bat last), the barnstormers were going to raise far more cash than they'd anticipated. Then this afternoon, with the higher-priced admission, food and beverage concession stands, and even more cranks in attendance, they had the opportunity to make hundreds and hundreds of dollars, more money than they'd earned at any other point on their cross-country adventure. To date, the team had raised only a little more than six hundred dollars. They were a long way from the ten thousand they needed. If all went well today, Ruby thought the Rough Riders could double their winnings.

But that was a mighty big if.

**CRANKS:** *fans, usually the hometown fans. Also called "rooters" (see page 303).*

Ruby looked over at her mother, standing with Scribe, Professor Lance, Preacher Wil, and Bubbles. Even as they worked the ticket table, they all kept a close eye on her and Graham. She and her brother were under strict orders not to wander away, and the only reason they had been permitted to stand apart from the adults was because the ballists were closely monitoring everyone who passed through the gate and onto the bridge.

Slipping her hand into her empty pocket, Ruby sighed. As hopeful and positive as she wanted to be, she had to be realistic. The Sprint Across the River was now moments away. But there was still no sign of Griffith, Woody, and Dog. And there was still no baseball.

Way in the distance, on the Illinois side of the St. Louis Bridge, Crazy Feet stepped to the starting line and positioned himself between his *two* opponents.

Yes, for this footrace, Crazy Feet would be pitted against a pair of St. Louis speedsters. The Superstars couldn't decide which *one* ballist should represent their team in the sprint, so they'd asked if *two* runners could compete. Since the hometowners had been so kind and hospitable, the Travelin' Nine were more than willing to accommodate the request.

"If you like," the Professor had said, "you can run your entire nine against Crazy Feet. It won't make a difference to him."

Ruby brushed the hair from her eyes and gazed out at the left scout's opponents. She'd seen both men at yesterday's practice, though she hadn't been formally introduced. To Crazy Feet's left stood Ed McKean, the fleet-footed shortstop from Ohio. Lave Cross, the speedy ballist who could play every position on the pitch, stood on his right.

"I see they're wearing their new red uniforms," said an unfamiliar voice from behind Ruby and Graham.

They turned. A man in a blue shirt, a yellow bowtie, and a light brown derby hat approached.

"Who are you?" asked Ruby, reflexively reaching for her brother.

"I'm a reporter," the man replied. He pointed to the notepad resting on the rim of his hat against the crown. "I work over at the *Globe*. I've been assigned to cover the race and the match. What brings you two out here today?"

Ruby drew Graham closer and glanced over at the others, just a few yards down the walkway. She was almost certain the man was a reporter, but she still needed to be cautious.

"Do you have a business card?" she asked. "Some form of identification? My mother doesn't like when we—"

"Whoa!" shouted the Professor, hustling over. The other players followed closely behind. "What do you want with these kids?"

"Here comes the cavalry!" the reporter remarked, holding up his hands. "No need for concern," he added, laughing. "Like I was telling these lovely little ones, I write for the *Globe*. I'm doing a story on the race." He pulled out a pen and then swung his head so that the notepad flew off his hat. He caught it with one hand. "I'd just pointed out to these two that the locals were wearing their red uniforms."

"What color do they usually wear?" Preacher Wil asked. He rested his hands on Graham's shoulders.

"Up until this season, our ballists wore brown. However, with the new owners and all these players arriving from Cleveland, the team changed colors." He leaned in and covered his mouth like he was telling a secret. "If you ask me, they look like a bunch of cardinals that flew—"

The reporter stopped midsentence. A boy wearing a baseball cap on sideways, who looked to be about Griffith's age, approached.

"Well, look who's here!" the reporter exclaimed. "It's Junior Lewis!"

"Who's Junior Lewis?" asked Ruby.

The reporter waved his pen like a wand at the crowd. "Ask any one of these fine folks," he replied, smiling, "and they'll tell you. They've never seen anyone run faster."

"Neither have I!" Junior Lewis declared. He placed both hands on his hips and stood up tall.

Peering out across the bridge, the reporter said, "Bet he could even beat that Crazy Feet fellow of yours."

"No way!" Graham fired back. "Crazy Feet doesn't lose footraces. Not to some boy."

The reporter stroked his chin. "You brave enough to put your money where your mouth is?"

Ruby laughed. "My brother's so poor he can't pay attention!"

Graham elbowed her in the side.

"We're not the betting kind," Preacher Wil explained. "When it comes to money, we don't play around."

"Tell you what I'll do," the reporter said, holding up his notepad. A ten-dollar coin note was taped to the back. "This is my emergency money. My editor makes me carry it wherever I go, in case I stumble across the story of the century and need it." He pulled the coin note off the pad and handed it to the Professor. "I'm so confident Junior Lewis will win this race, that I'll put this money up as his entry fee."

Ruby studied the reporter closely. She still believed the man was who he said he was, but she couldn't help but wonder if this was another one of the Chancellor's dirty tricks. Were they being duped?

"If Junior Lewis over here wins the race," the reporter said, "he wins all the money, just like any of the other competitors. But no matter the outcome, you still keep that ten dollars. What do you say?"

Once word spread that *the* Junior Lewis was joining the race, the already buzzing crowd roared with delight. Even if Crazy Feet, Lave Cross, Ed McKean, or anyone else had objected to the boy participating, they would've been overruled by the masses.

As the four speedsters lined up shoulder-to-shoulder-to-shoulder-to-shoulder on the far side of the St. Louis Bridge, Ruby wasn't concerned. Nor were any of the barnstorm-ers. Not only was Crazy Feet the fastest human they'd ever seen, but he was a skilled sprinter, too. He'd lost the pregame race back in Louisville because it was a dash around the bases, not a straight shot like this.

*"Go!"*

With the umpire's call, all four runners burst from the line. Junior Lewis got off to the fastest start, and by the time he reached the end of the first span, he was several yards ahead of the Superstar sprinters, who in turn, were several more yards ahead of Crazy Feet.

"Run!" Graham urged. "Faster!"

As the foursome dashed across the second span, Crazy Feet began to make his move. He blew by Ed McKean, who had fallen behind his teammate. Next, the

Travelin' Nine's left scout set his sights on Lave Cross.

"Here comes Crazy Feet!" Ruby called.

Lave Cross peeked nervously over his right shoulder as the runners headed across the third span. Crazy Feet was gaining ground! The Superstars' all-purpose player glanced back again, and as soon as he did,

Crazy Feet sailed past him on the left. By the time Lave Cross faced forward again, the Rough Rider was strides in front.

Crazy Feet now had only one more man— boy—to beat. Lowering his shoulders and raising his knees, he prepared for his final push.

"Watch this!" Graham announced.

If anyone in the crowd blinked an eye, they missed Crazy Feet's charge. Blazing by Junior Lewis, he never slowed down or looked back. The Rough Rider crossed the finish line so far ahead of the boy (and the others), he was already loosening his boots when they arrived.

"Crazy Feet won!" Ruby exclaimed.

"He did it!" cheered Graham.

The barnstormers raced over to their left scout, but Crazy Feet wasn't celebrating his victory. Instead he was grabbing his leg and grimacing.

"What's the matter?" Graham asked. "Did you hurt yourself?"

"You pull a hamstring?" Doc Lindy asked, noting that the Rough Rider was holding the back of his leg.

Crazy Feet nodded once.

Draping her arm around the left scout's shoulder, Ruby could tell he wanted to celebrate with his teammates, but his agony wouldn't allow it. She peered off into the general direction of the field on which they would be playing this afternoon. The last thing the Travelin' Nine could afford was an injured player. What would they do if . . .

Ruby stopped herself. Suddenly she realized Graham had been right. Without Griffith here, she had become the worrier.

Though she would never in a million years admit it to Graham.

# 10

★

## *Jump!*

**thought you said you couldn't**
sleep on trains." Woody chuckled.

"I can't," said Griffith.

"Could've fooled me! I reckon
I thought you were going to sleep the day
away!"

Across the boxcar, Woody and Truman
stood by the edge, staring out at the sun-
soaked countryside. The Rough Rider had
pushed the heavy doors all the way open,
and the fresh air poured in.

Griffith sat up and rubbed his eyes. He

had slept. And for quite a while, too. Gazing up at the sun high in the sky, Griffith figured it had to be almost noon. Maybe even later.

"We're just about in St. Louis," Woody spoke to the passing scenery.

Suddenly Griffith realized it was Saturday. Today was Graham's birthday. It was game day.

Rising to his feet, Griffith shuffled across the car. "You know where the match is, right?" he asked.

"'Course," Woody replied. "The field's located a little north of the city. Not too far from these tracks. First pitch is at one o'clock."

Like Happy and the Professor, Woody knew the Travelin' Nine's entire itinerary by heart. As soon as a match or travel plan was added to the schedule, Woody made a point of memorizing the details and particulars. The other ballists often relied on the right scout when they needed to know when and where they were going next. Especially Bubbles. No matter how many times the shortstop was told schedule information, he could never remember it.

"How long until we get to the station?" Griffith asked. He reached down and scratched behind Truman's floppy ears.

Woody thought for a moment. "An hour," he answered. "Perhaps two."

Griffith shook his head. "We don't have that kind of time."

"What choice do we have?"

"I have an idea."

"Am I going to like this idea?" Woody turned to Griffith.

Griffith smiled.

"I reckon I don't like the looks of *that*," Woody said. "If you're thinkin' what I think you're thinkin', the answer is no."

"Why not, Woody? It's our best option."

"It's not an option." Woody folded his arms. "Absolutely not."

"We're coming in from the north," said Griffith, "and you said the field is north of the city."

Woody stepped away from the open door. "I repeat, it's not an option."

"It's not like we haven't done it before," Griffith reasoned. "If we wait until the station, it could take us another two hours. Maybe more."

Woody shook his head again, though not as adamantly as he had moments ago.

"You know I'm right," Griffith pressed. He could tell the Rough Rider was starting to waver. "We need to jump off this train!"

Suddenly Griffith felt the knot in his stomach tighten. When he'd jumped off the train after Truman and the baseball, there hadn't been time to think. If there had been—even a moment or two—he probably would've lost his nerve and never have made the leap of faith. He stepped to the edge and stared at the ground speeding by. He *needed* to stop thinking.

"We're doing this," Griffith stated confidently.

Woody beat his bowlegs and then shuffled back over to Griffith. "I reckon your mother is goin' to have my head once she learns 'bout all the things I allowed you to do on this trip."

"Don't worry, Woody." Griffith rested a hand on the Rough Rider's shoulder. "I'll protect you."

Woody laughed. "I've seen your mother angry, Griff. An army led by your own pop couldn't protect me against her!"

Griffith smiled. He thought about his father and began to nod. In moments such as these, when so much was at stake, Griffith knew *exactly* what his father would do.

"We're doing this for the Travelin' Nine," he declared, dipping his hand into his pocket and gripping the baseball. "They need you to play in the game. They need us to help figure out who is betraying them. And we're doing this for my mother. She needs her family together. She needs to know the truth. We're doing this for Ruby, too. I can't leave her alone with Graham. He would drive her crazy." Griffith chuckled and then lifted the baseball out. "And we're doing this for Graham. We need to be there for his birthday. We need to protect him."

"You make quite a convincing case," said Woody. "You're beginnin' to sound a lot like someone I used to know." He reached over and placed his hand on the baseball.

As soon as he did, Truman lifted his front paw and placed it on their hands.

Both Woody and Griffith laughed.

"That's what I call a show of unity!" Woody

exclaimed. Then he pointed up ahead. "I reckon we're getting' closer to the river. The field should be just over those hills. You ready?"

"Ready as I'll ever be," replied Griffith.

"We wait till we reach that curve," Woody said, leaning out. "I'm hopin' this train slows some around the bend."

"Me too."

Woody clapped for the hound, who instantly sat down between them. "As soon as we pass this next set of trees, we're jumpin'."

"I'll go first," Griffith said.

Woody wagged a finger. "I appreciate your independence, but we're all committin' this act of stupidity—I mean, bravery—together."

"Any last pieces of advice?" Griffith spoke to the speeding ground.

"I have two," Woody replied. He beat his bowlegs again. "When we jump, we make sure we hit the ground feet first. Then we curl into balls and roll till we stop. So it's jump, hit, curl, roll. Got it?"

"Jump, hit, curl, roll," Griffith repeated. "Woody, that's *four* things."

"Four?" Woody rolled his broad shoulders. "That's only one. That was the first thing."

"Then what's the second thing?"

Woody smiled. "The second thing is actually the first thing."

"Huh?"

"The first thing is when we're fixin' to jump, we need to double-check to make sure there ain't no trees in the way or cliffs in sight." He patted Griffith on the shoulder and moved into leaping position. "Griff, I reckon it probably ain't the best idea in the world to tell your mother about this."

"I wasn't planning on it."

Suddenly Woody's face turned serious. "You ready?" he asked.

*"Jump!"*

"Jump, hit, curl, roll," said Griffith.

"Here we go. On three. One, two—"

"Wait!" Griffith grabbed Woody's arm. "Do we jump *on* three or *after* three?"

"I'm going to say one, two, three, jump. We jump on jump. Got that?"

Griffith clenched his fists. "Jump on jump."

"One, two, three . . . *jump!*"

# 11

★

*Together Again*

"uby!" **Griffith shouted** at the top of his lungs as he sped down the hill with Truman by his side. "Grammy!"

"We're here!" cried Woody, racing a few strides behind Griffith. "We made it!"

The barnstormers, led by Ruby and Graham, charged up the slope toward the returning trio.

"Griff!" Ruby called. "Woody!"

"I knew you'd make it back!" Graham

bolted by his sister. "I knew it all along!"

The two brothers were the first to reach each other. Jumping as high as they could, Griffith and Graham hugged in midair and tumbled to the turf. They rolled down the incline wrapped in each other's arms, while Truman nipped at their flailing limbs. When they finally stopped, Ruby and Elizabeth piled on.

"Happy birthday!" Griffith exclaimed as Truman licked his face.

"How did you get here?" Graham asked.

"Where have you been?" Ruby added.

"Did they hurt you?" Elizabeth nudged the hound aside, pointed him to Preacher Wil, and then kissed Griffith's forehead and cheeks.

As the Payne family rose to their feet, Woody headed for his teammates. Doc Lindy and Professor Lance greeted him with soldier salutes, Tales and Bubbles swatted him with their caps, and Happy (of all people) tried hoisting him off the ground.

Griffith stepped over to Preacher Wil, who'd knelt beside his loyal companion.

"His name's Truman," Griffith said.

Preacher Will glanced up at Griffith. "Truman?"

"He told me," Griffith said. "I mean, he didn't exactly tell me, but I—"

Preacher Wil held up his hand with the missing finger. "You don't have to explain," he said with his reassuring smile. "I understand." He shook the hound's head and then gazed into his eyes. "Truman it is."

"What's a Truman?" asked Graham, joining the conversation.

"He's Truman," Griffith replied, motioning to the hound. "That's his name. He told me."

"Told you?" Graham scrunched his face into a knot.

"I missed that ridiculous expression!" Griffith pointed at his brother and laughed.

"Told you?" Graham repeated, shaking his head. "I leave you alone for a few days, and you come back talking to animals!"

Griffith ruffled his brother's hair. It felt nice to be teased by Graham again (though he would never admit it).

"You have it, right?" Ruby asked Griffith.

Griffith nodded. He reached into his

pocket, removed the baseball, and held it high.

"Huzzah!" the Rough Riders cheered.

"Now I hate to be the one to ruin this remarkable reunion," the Professor said, holding up his hands, "but we need to go."

"I reckon we just got here," said Woody.

"Where were you going?" The smile left Griffith's face. "Were you leaving without us?"

**"HUZZAH!":** *common cheer to show appreciation for a team's effort.*

"'Course not!" Tales replied. "We weren't leaving St. Louis until you arrived. No matter how dangerous things got. But we couldn't stay at the field."

"What's going on?" asked Griffith.

"The game was canceled," Elizabeth said.

Griffith gasped. "Canceled?"

"What do you mean, canceled?" Woody asked, folding his arms. "Were the ballists here as disgraceful as the Millers?"

"It wasn't up to the Superstars," Ruby

replied. "They had nothing to do with it."

Professor Lance stepped forward. "Right before the start of the game," he explained, "several city officials notified everyone that the game had been called off. They read a statement *supposedly* from the mayor himself."

"The cranks were furious," Tales added. "Some started throwing fruit at the officials. One woman even hurled a shoe."

"The Superstars were angry too," Bubbles inserted.

"So was Graham!" the youngest Payne added.

"We all knew what was really happening," the Professor continued, motioning to the Rough Riders. "The Chancellor was up to more of his dirty tricks. Griff, in these parts, the Chancellor wields so much power and influence he can even sway local lawmakers." The Professor glanced back in the direction of the South First Street base-ball field. "He may try something else."

"That's why we need to be on our way to New Orleans," Elizabeth said.

"At least we have the money Crazy Feet earned from the footrace," Doc declared. He held up the cigar box containing the winnings. "There's a hundred and twenty dollars in here!"

Griffith looked to his mother. "Please don't tell me I have to get back on a train," he said.

"We're taking a boat," she said, smiling. "A steamer like the one we rode to Louisville." Elizabeth pulled Graham in closer. "And we're having a party. It's someone's birthday!"

# 12

★

## The Birthday Dinner

**heck out the size** of this room!" Graham exclaimed as he entered the festival hall with his brother and sister.

"We have it all to ourselves," said Ruby.

Upon boarding the steamboat, Happy and the Professor had met with the captain's assistant, hoping to secure a private space for Graham's birthday dinner. At best, they'd thought the barnstormers would be permitted to use a small dining room or a lounge.

However, to their surprise, the first mate granted them access to the grand ballroom below deck, since no events were scheduled there that evening.

"The birthday boy has arrived!" Griffith announced.

At the far end of the hall, the ballists were already seated at the long, rectangular dinner table. They all stood and raised their glasses when they saw the three Paynes heading toward them.

Walking across the enormous dance floor, Graham smiled wide as he gazed around the ballroom. A "Happy Birthday!" sign was suspended from the ceiling, while a "Huzzah!" banner was hung above the doorway to the kitchen.

"You're sitting at the head of the table," Elizabeth said with a smile. She locked her arm around her youngest son's arm and escorted him to the empty seat on the end.

Doc pulled out the chair, dusted it off with a napkin, and motioned for Graham to sit.

"This is how I should be treated at *every* meal," Graham said, beaming.

"I have a surprise for you, Grammy," said Elizabeth as the barnstormers returned to their seats. "I spoke with the chef earlier. When I told him it was your special day, he was kind enough to allow me to prepare your birthday dinner."

"A home-cooked meal for my birthday!"

Elizabeth smiled. "An *almost* home-cooked meal."

"Please tell me you made your macaroni and cheese," Graham said, bringing his hands together like he was praying.

Elizabeth's grin was her response.

Graham savored every last mouthful of his birthday meal. Of course, this celebration was much different from the ones he was used to. Back home, each year on the

Sunday before his birthday, family and friends would gather in the yard for a pig roast. Everyone spent the afternoon running races, competing in contests, and singing songs. This party may have been quieter and more subdued, but it was still enjoyable. Graham was surrounded by all the people who could be here.

"You were right, Griff," he said after cleaning off his plate.

"What was I right about?" Griffith asked.

Graham leaned in closer to his brother. "About Dad not coming back for my birthday. I was wrong."

Griffith nodded. "I wanted to believe it too, Grammy."

Folding his napkin, Griffith studied his brother closely. On the one hand, he was relieved that Graham finally understood their father would not be returning. But at the same time, Griffith still sensed a hint of confusion and disbelief. Did Graham really mean it? Or had his brother simply told him what he wanted to hear?

"I have another surprise for you, Grammy," Elizabeth announced once the table had been cleared. She motioned to Scribe, who headed into the kitchen. "It's a gift from the chef. He's already gone to bed, but he wanted you to have this."

"I know what it is!" Graham drumrolled the table.

A moment later Scribe emerged from the kitchen holding the most beautiful birthday cake Graham had ever seen. It was covered with white frosting, and the trim was made up of tiny chocolate baseballs. Across the top, the words HAPPY 8TH BIRTHDAY, GRAHAM! were written in bright blue cursive letters.

"Cakes are the chef's specialty," Elizabeth

explained as Scribe placed the magnificent creation on the table in front of Graham. "Not many eight-year-olds celebrate their birthday on his boat, so he wanted to help make yours extra special."

"This is already turning into the *specialest* birthday ever!" Graham exclaimed.

Griffith gazed around at the group as they admired the dessert. The people here were his family.

But one of them couldn't be trusted.

He glanced to Truman, lying on the floor behind Preacher Wil's chair, and he was struck again by the sickening feeling he'd had back in Minneapolis and several times since. There was cause for concern about Truman; he knew there was. Griffith smiled at the hound anyway, and Truman appeared to smile back.

• • •

With his free hand, Griffith reached down, dipped two fingers into the lettering on the cake, and then painted a blue icing mustache on Graham's face.

"Happy birthday, Grams!"

"Huzzah!" everyone cheered.

"Time to dig in!" Graham exclaimed.

"Not so fast," said Elizabeth, standing up. "I still have one more surprise for you."

"You're really going to like this one," Bubbles said.

Elizabeth walked over to the corner of the ballroom. From underneath the platform where musical instruments were set up— instruments Graham hadn't even noticed until now—she removed a large box. She returned to the table and placed it beside the birthday cake.

"Do you have any idea what it is?" Tales asked, twirling one end of his bushy mustache.

"Not at all." Slowly Graham lifted the cover and peeked in. His eyes popped. He reached around to his mother and hugged her as tight as he could. Then he opened the box all the way and removed a Travelin' Nine jersey and cap.

"This is for me?" he asked.

"Who else do you think it's for?" Preacher Wil laughed.

Graham placed the hat on his head and held up the uniform top. "Can I wear it to practices and games?"

"We hope you will," said Doc.

"It fits me?" Graham said to his mother.

"Of course it does," she replied. "I've been sewing that uniform ever since Chicago."

"That's what you've been working on?" Graham asked.

Elizabeth laughed. "Sometimes you were sitting next to me!"

"I thought you were repairing a jersey and—"

At the far end of the ballroom, six men wearing matching white suits and red vests walked in. For a split second, the barnstormers feared the worst, but their fears vanished almost instantly.

"We didn't know anyone was in here," said a man twirling drumsticks.

"We got a big gig comin' up this Wednesday down on Frenchmen Street," said a second man with a banjo around his neck.

"We wanted to rehearse," added a third. He pointed to the instruments in the corner.

"Can we listen?" Graham asked.

"Listen, sing, dance," said the man with the drumsticks. "We'd love it if you stuck around for our dress rehearsal."

Moments later the six-man jazz band was jamming, and the barnstormers were dancing. They formed a rowdy circle in the middle of the floor and spun wildly around the room. Even Happy danced, despite his weakened condition. So did Crazy Feet, though he took

It felt as if he was riding a bucking bronco.

things slightly slower because of his hurt hamstring.

"Time to give the birthday boy a ride!" Doc declared.

Suddenly Scribe was dragging a chair onto the dance floor, and with the help of Doc (not that Scribe needed help), they were hoisting Graham over their heads. They lifted him so high that he had to duck to avoid the crystal chandelier. For Graham, it felt as if he was riding a bucking bronco. When he wasn't holding on for dear life, he waved his new Travelin' Nine cap like a cowboy readying to lasso a calf.

# 13

★

## *Piecing the Pieces*

**O** **n the deck of the** steamer, Griffith, Ruby, Graham, and Truman sat in front of the large wooden storage bin filled with ropes, buoys, and safety equipment.

"So in the last few days," Graham said, "you've jumped off a moving train, jumped onto a moving train, and jumped off *another* moving train."

"And I walked about fifteen miles!" Griffith added, rubbing his shoes. "My feet and legs are going to be sore for weeks."

"Well, it's going to take me at least that long to come to terms with the fact that the Chancellor is Josiah's son," said Ruby.

Griffith tilted his head back and shielded his eyes from the sun high overhead. It was already afternoon. Their mother had let them sleep late. In fact, she'd insisted on it.

"Travel takes a toll on the body," she'd said as they went to bed after Graham's party. "I want you refreshed and ready for these last few weeks of the trip."

When Happy woke the three Paynes shortly before noon, he informed them that they'd be switching steamers in a short while. That had always been part of the plan. Because they were concerned about the Chancellor, the barnstormers needed to change boats during the journey to New Orleans. As a result, the trip down the Mississippi would take a little longer than usual, and they wouldn't arrive in the Crescent City, where they'd be staying at Happy's house, until first thing Monday morning.

So as they waited to move to the next vessel, Griffith brought his brother and sister up to speed. He told them everything Woody had described to him, starting with the long training days in San Antonio and the incident with Colonel Roosevelt and their baseball at the Menger Hotel and ending with everything that happened on San Juan Hill: Uncle Owen got shot *twice,* Doc Lindy appeared from out of the blue, and time stood still.

As Griffith spoke of bullets suspended motionless in flight and their father moving them about, Graham could barely breathe. What his brother described was *identical* to what he'd experienced during the seventh-inning snowstorm back in

Minneapolis. Maybe it hadn't been a dream after all. Maybe Graham really had seen his father.

But he was too stunned to share these thoughts with his brother and sister. Nor did he have the chance to.

"Let's go, kids," Doc called, appearing on the staircase farther down the deck.

"We're in Vicksburg?" Griffith asked. That was where the team was scheduled to make the transfer.

"Ten minutes," he replied. "Time to gather your belongings."

Once again, the three Paynes and Truman sat together on a steamer. This time they huddled around Ruby's open journal along the railing of the middle deck.

When switching boats, the Rough Riders searched each level of the floating palace. Only after they were certain there was no sign of the Chancellor or his thugs, the barnstormers met in the ship's cafeteria for a late-afternoon lunch. Upon finishing the meal, the ballists went their separate ways—some napped, some read, some chatted, one wrote. Griffith, Ruby, and Graham picked up where they'd left off.

"I've made separate pages for all of the ballists," Ruby explained to her brothers. "I've been writing down thoughts and facts and questions about each of them. I'm hoping my notes will help us narrow down the suspects."

"Well, we know it's not Woody," said Griffith, tapping the page with the right scout's name at the top. "I've explained to you why."

Ruby drew a large *X* across the paper. "It's not Scribe, either," she said, flipping back to his page, which already had an *X*.

"That leaves seven suspects," Graham counted.

"So we're including Preacher Wil?" Ruby asked. She felt the baseball over her pocket.

"We have to," replied Griffith. He glanced at Truman, whose head was yet again resting on his leg. The hound was choosing to be by their side almost all the time now. "Until we know for certain that Preacher Wil isn't the traitor," he added, "we have no choice but to include him."

"Let's see what you've written so far," Graham said.

Ruby opened to Doc Lindy's page and spun the notebook around to her brothers.

_Doc Lindy_

*not an original Rough Rider/not in San Antonio

*Didn't meet the others until moments after Uncle Owen had been shot

*Arrived from out of nowhere (too convenient?)

*Long dark beard (a disguise?)

"It sounds like he could be the one," Graham noted.

"I know." Ruby nodded and frowned.

"What did you write for Bubbles?" asked Griffith.

She flipped ahead a few pages.

Bubbles
   *Likes to make up stories
   *Others always ask him if he's telling the truth
   *Who are those distant relatives he talks about from Dayton, and what type of contraption are they really building?
   *During some of the games, not "setting the table" (see Crazy Feet)

"It sounds like he could be the one too," Graham said, holding his head.

"I know," Ruby repeated. "Read what I wrote about Crazy Feet."

_Crazy Feet_
  *Has not a said a single word
  *Always keeps his hat over his face/
never see his eyes
  *Lost the footrace in Louisville
  *During some of the games, not
"setting the table" (see Bubbles)

"They all sound guilty," Griffith declared.

"That's the problem," Ruby agreed, still frowning.

"But I'm sure we could just as easily make a case why each Rough Rider _isn't_ the suspect," said Griffith.

"That's the problem too," she said.

"I have an idea," said Griffith. "Let's each pick one of the players and say why we think it might be him."

Ruby stood up and walked over to the railing. She rested her chin on the top bar and faced the river. "I don't want to do this," she muttered.

"Maybe what you've written down isn't enough," Griffith pressed. "Perhaps if we talk about what you've written, something will come to us."

"Fine," said Graham. "I'll go first. I pick Truman."

The hound lifted his head. His floppy ears perked up.

"Truman's working for the Chancellor," Graham said. "He *talks* to him just like he *talks* to you." Graham laughed. "What do you think, Truman? Are you the one?"

"You think you're funny, don't you?" Griffith made a face.

Graham smiled his mischievous smile. "Hilarious."

"I think Tales is the turncoat," Ruby blurted.

Griffith gasped. "You do?"

Ruby turned back to her brothers and flipped the hair off her neck. "No. I was just saying a name to get this over with."

"I think it's Professor Lance," Graham added.

"You're just saying that, too, right?" asked Griffith.

Graham nodded.

Griffith grabbed the back of his head. "This isn't going very well."

"Not at all," Ruby agreed, slipping her hand into her pocket and squeezing the baseball. "It's frustrating and discouraging. We should stop."

"What do you want to do instead?" Graham asked.

"Well, I want to write in my journal," Ruby answered. "That usually helps me feel better."

"Let's have a catch." Graham looked to Griffith.

"As long as you promise not to throw any balls overboard." Griffith wagged a finger at his brother.

"I make no such promises."

"But we do need to talk again," said Ruby.

"After dinner," Graham said.

Ruby shook her head. "I'm going straight to bed after dinner. I can't face it tonight. In the morning."

"We should wake up early and watch the sun rise as we pull into New Orleans," Griffith suggested.

"I like that idea," agreed Ruby.

"I'll ask the Professor to make sure we're up. He's always the first one awake."

"We should watch it from upstairs," Graham said, motioning above the deck. "The view will be better."

"That's exactly what I was thinking," said Griffith.

Graham beamed. "Great minds think alike!"

Griffith, Ruby, and Graham stood along the railing of the top deck of the steamboat.

All three were awestruck by the beautiful colors—red, pink, orange, and yellow—that were filling the horizon to the east and growing brighter by the second.

"I still can't believe the Chancellor is Josiah's son," Ruby said without lifting her chin from the railing. "He must feel terrible."

Griffith's chin remained on the railing too. "Josiah knows the Chancellor has to be stopped," he said. "He only hopes he's not too late."

"What happens if he is too late?" Ruby asked.

"He's not," Griffith replied flatly.

"But what if he is, Griff?"

"I can't allow myself to think that he is." Griffith glanced at Graham standing to his left. "I refuse to believe it."

While Graham could hear everything his brother and sister were saying, he couldn't

He didn't want to get their hopes up.

stop thinking about what Griffith had said about time standing still in Cuba. At several points—while playing catch, during dinner, and before going to sleep—Graham had almost told his brother and sister what he'd experienced. But he didn't want to get their hopes up. Or his own.

As the sun cleared the trees in the east, the magnificent Crescent City came into full view. Hundreds of piers and scores of vessels of all shapes and sizes filled the waters. Large warehouses, factories, and buildings lined both shores. And off in the distance, the faint sounds of music, not unlike what the band had played during Graham's birthday party, could be heard.

The steamer wound around one final bend, heading for the empty pier nestled among all the other floating palaces. When the boat began to dock, Griffith, Ruby, Graham, and Truman trotted to the front. They wanted to see everything first.

# 14

★

*A Relative Returns*

e must go!"
Uncle Owen
announced. "This
wharf is not safe."

"The Chancellor
and his men are here?" Ruby asked.

Uncle Owen shook. "Everyone knows
about the Chancellor?" He peered around at
the Travelin' Nine.

Griffith, Ruby, and Graham had been the
first ones off the steamboat. As soon as the
mooring lines had been fastened to the pier,

they'd raced down the ramp toward their uncle. When they reached him, he was back in his wheelchair, and up close, he looked frailer than ever, with a hollowed-out face, sunken eyes, and skeleton-like arms. Only Ruby dared to touch him, kissing him gently on the cheek.

But to Ruby, her uncle's sickly appearance wasn't what she found to be most disturbing. It was the large bruise that covered half of his forehead and the long gash that ran along his neck that terrified her. Gazing at the ballists, she sensed that was what concerned them as well.

"I've arranged for transportation back to Happy's," said Uncle Owen, his voice quivering like it had when he'd greeted his brother's family and his fellow Rough Riders, and introduced himself to Preacher Wil.

"Are we taking a streetcar there?" Griffith asked. "Happy said the electric one runs right out to—"

Uncle Owen pointed to three horse-drawn wagons filled with crates of fruit at the end of the pier.

"How are we all going to fit?" asked Graham.

"We'll split up," Uncle Owen replied. He covered his body-shaking cough with a rail-thin forearm. "Everyone will need to hide under the tarps." He labored to swallow. "We mustn't let them see us."

"This cannot wait," Bubbles said as the barnstormers headed up the front steps into Happy's home. He glared at Owen. "We need to discuss things now."

"I agree," the Professor added, his eye focused on the wounded veteran. "I call a team meeting."

Griffith stared at his uncle too. Without a doubt, Uncle Owen was aware of the sharp glances and simmering tensions. Even Scribe and Crazy Feet, who at the moment

were helping him up the stairs, looked at
him with disgust.

"We can convene in the room down the
hall," Happy said. "However, I suggest we ask
the children to wait outside, either in the yard
or the kitchen. Some of the things that may
be said . . . it may not be appropriate for them
to be there."

Griffith peered at his mother, standing in
the doorway with pursed lips and balled fists
of fury. She couldn't even look in her brother-
in-law's direction.

"No," Elizabeth said, her voice without
emotion. She shook her head. "My children
need to be there. I want them in my sights."
She then turned to Owen. "I want them to
hear what their uncle has to say."

In Happy's living room, all the barnstormers
gathered in a circle. Griffith, Ruby, and
Graham sat on cushions on the parquet

wood floor, while the adults sat on armchairs, ottomans, and dining chairs. Uncle Owen remained in his wheelchair.

"Let's get right down to business," the Professor said, once everyone had settled in.

"I reckon Owen has a lot of explainin' to do," said Woody, his arms folded tightly across his chest and his eyes fixed on the Rough Rider who had just returned.

"We're waiting," Tales added.

Owen's frail frame shuddered as he let out a deep breath. "The terms of the debt have changed," he said, speaking slowly. "The money is no longer due at the end of the century." He ran his hand across the purple and yellow bruise on his forehead and then rested it on his stump. "A down payment is expected by the end of the month."

Ruby covered her frown and then glanced up at her mother, seated between Happy and Doc. Elizabeth's fists were still clenched. It was only a matter of time before she *erupted*.

"But the end of the month is this Thursday," Woody noted.

Uncle Owen grimaced. "We need to pay twenty percent by Thursday. The bank wants—"

"That's two thousand dollars!" Tales exclaimed.

"I've had it, Owen!" shouted Elizabeth suddenly. "I am tired of the lies. This has gone on long enough." She rose from her seat. "We're all tired of the lies. Everyone in this room knows they are lies." She pointed to Griffith, Ruby, and Graham. "Even your brother's children know it." She crossed her arms and glared at Owen. "When are they going to stop? *When?*"

Owen's eyes flitted from adult to adult, never resting on one for more than a moment. He never lowered his gaze, either; he didn't have the courage to look at his niece and nephews.

Ruby chewed on her lower lip as she focused on Uncle Owen's hand, still resting on his stump. Was he rubbing it?

"You are embarrassing yourself." Elizabeth stepped toward her brother-in-law and pointed down at him. "We all know about the Chancellor, Owen Payne. For once in your life, tell the truth!"

Griffith shook. He reached for Graham's hand. His brother was trembling just like he was. Then Griffith looked to Ruby. She was clutching Graham's other hand, holding it so tight that her knuckles had whitened. Finally Griffith glanced down at Truman, who lay in front of his crossed legs. Even the hound had nestled closer.

"Two thousand dollars must be paid by Thursday," Uncle Owen finally said, his eyes shut and shoulders sagging. "If we don't come up with that money, the debt is accelerated."

"Accelerated?" asked Tales, twirling one

end of his bushy mustache. "What does that mean?"

"We don't have that kind of coin yet," Bubbles said, inching forward in his seat. "Even with Crazy Feet's winnings from the footrace, we only have seven or eight hundred dollars."

"If we fail to come up with the money by Thursday," Owen interrupted, "all the money—the full amount—will be due at the end of September." His eyes remained closed. "Ten thousand dollars will need to be repaid not by the end of the century, but by the end of next month."

Griffith gazed back at his mother. Even though she was seated again, her furious and unblinking eyes remained focused on her husband's brother. Then Griffith looked at the other adults. Doc chomped on his tongue, Scribe gnawed on his knuckle, and the Professor tugged on the cord of his eye patch. Griffith could *taste* the Rough Riders' anger at the Chancellor and their disappointment in Uncle Owen.

"Why did you tell the kids to keep the baseball a secret?" Tales asked.

"Why couldn't *we* know they had it?" Bubbles pressed, running his fingers along what remained of his left ear.

Wincing, Uncle Owen opened his eyes, looked at his niece and nephews, and nodded.

Griffith nodded back and then watched as Truman slowly rose to his paws and hobbled across the wood floor to Uncle Owen. The hound lay down in front of the wheelchair. It was as if Truman was trying to tell Uncle Owen *he* had forgiven him. Griffith smiled and sighed. He understood that his uncle was finished answering questions, at least for now.

As angry as they were, the Rough Riders realized it as well.

"I think it's time for Owen to get some rest," the Professor said, standing up. "We can continue this discussion later in the day."

"I reckon that's fine by me," said Woody, "so long as he understands this conversation isn't over."

"I do," Owen whispered. He faced Elizabeth. "I know this may ring hollow, but in the presence of everyone, I'd like to apologize to my brother's wife." He placed his hand against the bruise on his forehead. "I'm so sorry, Elizabeth. For all that I've done, for all that I've put you through."

The barnstormers waited for a response, but Elizabeth offered none. Her angry eyes remained fixed on Owen.

"I do have one piece of hopeful news," Uncle Owen said, breaking the silence. "I've arranged for not one, but two days of baseball against the local team. A two-day festival."

"We can raise more money!" Graham cheered.

"That we can." Uncle Owen managed his first smile of the afternoon. "The opening day of the festival will be a day of contests. The second day will be the match."

"When is the festival?" Ruby asked.

"Friday and Saturday."

Ruby bowed her head.

"Friday is September first," Doc noted. "That's after the end of the month."

"We won't have the money in time," said the Professor.

"But we'll make a lot of money," Griffith said, a trace of defiance in his tone. He stood up and stepped over to his uncle. "It will put us on the path for the money we need by September thirtieth." He glanced down at Truman before placing his hand on top of Uncle Owen's, which rested on the wheelchair's arm. "We will pay off this debt. No matter what the amount. No matter what it takes."

# 15

★

## Uncle Owen and the Chancellor

**ith the meeting** adjourned, Griffith, Ruby, and Graham helped Uncle Owen to a bedroom in the back of the house. While all the others opted for rooms on the second and third floors, Owen selected one on the main level so that he wouldn't have to navigate stairs in his wheelchair.

"I'd like to speak to the three of you now," he said as Griffith and Ruby helped him onto his bed.

"No," Griffith said. "The Professor was right. You need your rest."

"You should sleep," added Graham. "We'll talk in the morning."

Uncle Owen managed a smile. "As long as you like," he whispered, lowering his head to his pillow.

Annoyed, Ruby looked away. She didn't agree with Griffith. She wanted to have the conversation now and was surprised that Graham had gone along with him. Ruby wasn't used to seeing her younger brother show patience. But in her heart, she knew they were right. At the moment, Uncle Owen was far too drained to do anything.

The three siblings spent the afternoon exploring Happy's home.

The house was enormous. The ground floor had a restaurant-size kitchen, a dining room with a birch-wood table big enough

for all the barnstormers to sit around simultaneously, a living room (where the team
meeting had been held), and several sitting
areas. The second and third floors contained
multiple bedrooms. Each room also had
a balcony, while the first floor had a wrap-
around porch with rocking chairs, flower
boxes, and a three-person porch swing. But
the most striking feature of all at the front
of the house were the five mammoth white-
painted columns, which looked like the ones

in their father's book about ancient Greece.

Griffith, Ruby, and Graham were amazed that Happy owned such a *castle*. So were the Rough Riders. Happy explained that it used to belong to his mother, and when she passed, she'd left the home to him, her only offspring. Unfortunately, he was unable to afford such a house, and maintaining it was costing him what little savings he had to his name. But Happy couldn't get himself to part with this last remaining connection to his mother.

By the time the three Paynes finished exploring and then eating, they were exhausted (after all, their day had started before sunrise on the boat). None of them put up any resistance when their mother said it was time for sleep, especially since it had started to rain and they couldn't play outside.

The next morning they were up bright and early. They made sure Uncle Owen was too. Like he'd promised, he was ready to talk, and he wanted to start even before break- fast. Griffith, Ruby, and Graham helped their uncle get dressed, lifted him into his chair, and wheeled him to the front porch.

Which was where they all sat now.

Griffith peered out at the yard. He wanted this conversation to take place underneath the two massive live oaks in the middle of the lawn, away from thin walls and open win- dows. But the rainstorm wouldn't allow it. He flicked the droplets from his brow. So much about this moment reminded Griffith of the afternoon of his father's funeral: the driving sheets of rain and gale-force gusts; Uncle Owen never looking worse; and the four of them gathered outside to discuss matters of grave importance.

"I'm no longer worthy to hold the base- ball," Uncle Owen said.

"Yes, you are," said Ruby, placing it in his

hand and closing his fingers around it.

"I'm the reason the Chancellor knows of you," he whispered, directing his words to Graham.

"How does he know about me?" Graham asked.

"Because I gamble."

"What does that have to do with the Chancellor?" Graham wondered, glancing at Griffith, who sat to his left on the porch swing.

"I play cards, Graham. Always have. I was a card player before the war and a card player after." Uncle Owen sighed. "It was my playing after Cuba that got me into this mess. Forced me to borrow money to pay my debts." He sighed again. "I'd gotten jammed up a few times as a younger man, but never like this. Never like this." He thumped his chest with the baseball as he cleared his throat. "What I didn't know was that the man I borrowed the money from had ties to the Chancellor. If I'd known it, I never would have. Never. I swear."

Griffith looked to Ruby. She sat beside Uncle Owen in a mustard-colored rocking chair with oversize armrests. She was rocking back and forth, keeping time with her uncle's words. When he slowed, she slowed. When he paused, she stopped. Griffith wondered if Ruby even realized she was doing this.

"My debts grew larger," Uncle Owen continued. "Hundreds of dollars became hundreds and hundreds of dollars, and before I knew it—"

"Why didn't you just stop, Uncle O?" Graham interrupted.

Uncle Owen swallowed. "Because I gamble," he repeated, his voice filled with resignation.

Griffith glanced over at his brother and smiled. Graham was asking all the right questions. Griffith couldn't get over how much he'd grown up these last few weeks.

"It's always been my weakness, my failing as a human being." Uncle Owen lowered his head and spoke to the baseball he cradled against his emaciated frame. "Just needed one more hand, one good night, one solid run of luck. That's what I kept telling myself. Like I always did. But it never happened. Never. And I never learned. The chase never stopped." Uncle Owen looked up. "One day, the man I borrowed all the money from showed up at the lounge. But he was no longer alone. Three others were with him, and the moment I saw their dark suits and pocket squares, I knew exactly who they were. All of us sitting around that table did. But they didn't come to demand money." Uncle Owen shook his head and fixed his stare on Graham. "They were demanding you."

"How did they know about me?" Graham asked again.

"Loose lips," Uncle Owen replied. The ends of his mouth turned downward. "Often when I played cards, I drank. It impaired my judgment, contributed to my losing, and made me foolish." He pressed two fingers to his temple. "From time to time, I said things I shouldn't have. Spoke of your abilities. Bragged about them, in fact. But I never mentioned you by name. Never. I just said I knew of a baseball prodigy like no other."

"And someone from the card game told the Chancellor?" Ruby asked.

Uncle Owen placed the baseball in his lap and reached for the washcloth in the basin hooked to his armrest. But his trembling fingers couldn't hold on to it.

"Let me," said Ruby. She inched forward in the rocker, put the baseball into her pocket, and picked up the cloth.

"News filtered back to the Chancellor," Uncle Owen said, his eyes closed while Ruby wiped his brow. "He has a way of learning about everything. And then one day he showed up. Not to the card game, but to my front door." He opened his eyes and faced Graham again. "The Chancellor had two of his men with him, and they just walked right in and demanded the prodigy of whom I'd spoken. Of course I was terrified, but I refused to reveal your identity. I even tried to say I made the whole thing up, but that only made him angrier."

"So what did you do?" Graham's eyes widened.

"I offered money," Uncle Owen replied. "An absurd amount of money. I knew the Chancellor was driven by greed and—"

"But you didn't have any money!" Griffith interrupted.

Uncle Owen frowned. "No, I didn't. And

the Chancellor knew it too. So he responded in kind. He demanded several times the amount I'd offered. Ten thousand dollars. And he said he'd be back in one week's time to collect it." Uncle Owen swallowed. "He said if I had his money upon his return, he would leave me to live my life and cease his pursuit of the prodigy. I had no choice but to accept this proposal."

"But you didn't have any money," Griffith repeated. He hopped off the swing and walked over to the porch railing. "Why would he even bother to make such a proposal?"

"Better yet," Ruby said, "why didn't *you* just go to the police?"

"Ruby," said Uncle Owen, shaking his head, "I'm afraid that's not how things work. The Chancellor's not the type of person you go to the police about."

"So what happened a week later?" she asked. "Why did the Chancellor end up giving you until the end of the year to get the money?"

"The accident," Uncle Owen replied. He rolled his neck, took a deep breath, and lowered a hand to where his leg used to be. "After your father's untimely death, I think even the Chancellor showed some humanity. He didn't want to seem heartless and unreasonable. So he gave me until the end of the year."

Ruby turned to the pouring rain. Uncle Owen had rubbed his stump, and at the moment, she couldn't look at him. On the one hand, she couldn't stand the sight of him. How dare he continue to lie? But at the same time, she didn't have the heart to let him see the rage and disappointment on her face.

"What about the letter?" Griffith asked. He sat back down on the porch swing next to his brother. "Why did it arrive looking like that? What happened to it?"

"What happened to you?" Ruby added,

without looking back. "You're still not telling us everything."

"After you left for Cincinnati," Uncle Owen answered, running his fingers across the gash, "the Chancellor's men paid me a visit. Gave me a brutal beating."

"Why did they beat you up?" asked Graham.

Uncle Owen smiled bitterly. "Because they could. They were reminding me that the Chancellor always gets his way." He shook his head. "They taunted me during that beating. Told me the Travelin' Nine's baseball plan would never succeed." Uncle Owen rolled his chair closer to Griffith and Graham. "That's when I first learned one of the Rough Riders was working for the Chancellor."

"You knew?" Griffith smacked the back of the swing. "How could you not tell us?"

"Wait," Uncle Owen said, lifting a hand. "Let me explain."

"You'd better!" Ruby snarled.

Uncle Owen bristled.

So did Ruby. The words that had left her lips surprised even her. She whirled around and looked at him crossly, no longer concerned with sparing him the sight of her anger.

"How could you do this to us?" she asked.

"Right after the beating"—Uncle Owen's voice trembled— "I sent you the letter. That's why it looked like that."

"But it didn't say much."

"I explained everything about the turn-coat on the Travelin' Nine. I did. But the entire letter never made it to the envelope. After their visit, I was in such bad shape . . ." Uncle Owen placed a hand against his chest. "I only sent one page. I didn't realize it."

"I'm sorry for snapping, Uncle Owen," Ruby said, brushing the hair from her eyes and then reaching for his hand. "I should never speak to you so disrespectfully. I feel—"

"No, Ruby," he interrupted. He squeezed her fingers. "Don't apologize. I don't deserve apologies."

"What happened to the other page?" Graham asked.

Uncle Owen slowly rolled his shoulders. "If not for the Chancellor's thugs, I never would've learned I didn't send it. They paid me another visit the next week. They didn't rough me up nearly as bad as the first time, but it's how I got these cuts and bruises." He motioned to his face. "They left me lying on my bedroom floor, and that's when I discovered the rest of the letter. Underneath my bed. Inches from my slipper." He nodded. "I must've dropped it when I wrote it, and it drifted under the bed. As soon as I found it, I knew—"

"Do you know who the traitor is?" Graham asked.

"Not yet," Uncle Owen replied, shaking

his head, "but now that I'm here, I'm sure it won't take me long to figure that out."

Ruby laughed. "Good luck," she said skeptically. "It's not as easy as you think."

Uncle Owen squeezed her fingers again. "These last few weeks have been the most difficult of my life. All I could think about was you kids and the terrible danger you faced. But each morning I'd wake up, and I couldn't even muster the strength to get out of bed." He rubbed eyes that had begun to water. "Finally I told myself I had to try. Even if it meant losing my life. No matter the cost, I had to reach you."

"How did you get here without any money?" Graham asked. He knelt in front of the wheelchair, lifted the washcloth from the basin, and dabbed his uncle's face just like Ruby had a short time ago.

"A man does what he needs to do," Uncle Owen replied. He tilted his head back so

Graham could wipe his chin. "Believe it or not, this old wreck still had a few pennies left to his name. At least enough to get me to New Orleans." He gazed out into the yard at the driving rain. "A storm's blown into town. It knows no mercy, and I am responsible. I made my own brother, Guy Payne . . ." Uncle Owen's voice trailed off. "I've hurt so many people and caused unimaginable pain. For that, I will never forgive myself. Never."

Graham placed the cloth back into the basin and stood up. He then carefully draped his arm around his uncle and stared out at the swaying limbs of the live oaks.

"I thought my dad was coming back for my birthday, Uncle O," Graham said, speaking to the storm. "But everyone told me it couldn't happen."

"No, it couldn't," said his uncle.

"I guess it was really you who was coming."

"I guess . . . I guess that's true." He slid his hand from his armrest to his stump. "I'm suddenly very tired again. I need to return to bed." He cleared his throat. "But before I do, there's one more thing. There's something I must give you." He directed his words to Ruby.

"What is it?" she asked.

"Take the keys from around my neck," he instructed. "I need for you to have them."

"Why?" Ruby stepped closer.

"In case . . . I want them to be in your possession. Take them."

Ruby carefully reached behind her uncle's head and dipped her hands under his collar. She gently lifted the chain of keys from around his neck and then placed it around her own.

She knew what the keys unlocked. So did her brothers. Only she didn't know why he wanted her to have them.

# 16

★

## *Practice*

**S**itting in his wheel-chair on an incline behind the third bag line and surrounded by his brother's children, Uncle Owen beamed as he watched the Travelin' Nine on the practice field.

**BAG:** base. Also called "sack" (see page 85).

After speaking with his niece and nephews early in the morning, Owen had met with his fellow Rough Riders again, this time without the children present. For well over an hour, the soldiers confronted him, asking him all the questions they hadn't been able to the day before.

The grilling left him exhausted, in addition to sad and guilty. But for the moment he had baseball, the wonderful distraction.

"They've gotten good, haven't they?" Ruby said, smiling. She stood directly behind her uncle's chair with her hands resting on the handles.

"Indeed," said Uncle Owen. "I must say I'm amazed."

"You should see them in a game," Griffith said. "They play even better."

"Thanks to us!" Graham added. He reached back and patted the baseball in Ruby's pocket.

"They look like they can hold their own against anyone." Uncle Owen's voice was filled with hope.

"They sure can." Ruby squeezed the baseball. "No matter what the Chancellor tries." She leaned over and kissed the top of her uncle's head.

Despite what he had done and even though he had his flaws, Ruby loved having her uncle here. He had a good heart, which was why he reminded her so much of her father.

She glanced to Griffith, who was scanning the area beyond left garden. Since arriving at the practice field, all four of them had kept one eye on the action and one eye on everything else.

Just like Happy.

Happy wasn't sitting with them. At the moment, he was halfway down the right garden line. He'd been moving about all afternoon, constantly changing his vantage point, similar to the way the three Payne kids had during the match in Minneapolis. Happy was taking no chances.

Earlier in the day, Elizabeth, the Professor, and Scribe had all been concerned that the Chancellor might try something on their way to the field. So instead of heading straight to the practice area adjacent to Crescent City Base Ball Park, the team took a roundabout route—first on streetcars through the Garden District, then in wagons, and the rest of the way on foot. The trip, less than three miles, took twice as long as it should have.

But so far, there had been no sign of the Chancellor and his men.

Nor had Uncle Owen been able to detect any clues that would help his niece and nephews figure out who the mole was.

"This isn't as easy as I thought it would be," he conceded.

"That's what we've been trying to tell you," Ruby said.

She gazed out at the field. Even though it was sunny and the torrential rains had stopped early yesterday evening, the pitch was still waterlogged. When the ballists ran across the outfield grass, water sprayed from their boots. The infield dirt was strewn with puddles. Truman had found the largest one of all. He sat tall in the pond-size pool next to the mound, while Preacher Wil hurled batting practice.

Griffith studied Tales at the dish. The Travelin' Nine's second sack man was trying to drive all of Preacher Wil's offerings to the right side of the field. He stepped off the line to swing at the inside pitches and leaned over the dish for the outside ones. Griffith knew that a successful table setter needed to have excellent bat control, but he'd never realized just how hard Tales worked at perfecting the craft.

Crazy Feet batted next. After spraying a few balls to various parts of the field, he also started directing his hits toward right garden. Griffith wondered if this was a strategy the ballists had discussed prior to taking batting practice. With Crazy Feet's speed and a soggy,

**TABLE SETTER:** *Sometimes the first two batters in the lineup are called the "table setters." They "set the table" for all the other strikers in the batting order by getting on base.*

rain-soaked playing surface, any base hit to right garden could be a double, and shots down the line were potential three baggers.

Now Scribe headed to the dish, but before he reached the plate, Preacher Wil stepped off the bump. The hurler was distracted by a group of men in baseball uniforms approaching from behind first bag.

Everyone turned.

"I think the Pelicans are here," said Ruby.

The New Orleans Pelicans was the team the Travelin' Nine were slated to compete against in the baseball festival.

**THREE BAGGER:** *triple.*

"I hope they're a bunch of friendly birds," Graham quipped.

Griffith nodded. "You and me both, little brother."

The Rough Riders, led by Happy, headed for the hometown ballists gathering near the dish. As Ruby rolled her uncle onto the pitch, she held her breath. Were they going to be friendly? Would they object to the color of Preacher Wil's skin? How were they going to react if . . . ?

"Greetin's, y'all," said one of the players. He doffed his cap. "Some of the fellas heard y'all were playin' out here today, so we figured we'd come on out and welcome you to our city. Show y'all some Southern hospitality."

"We're the Travelin' Nine," Happy introduced the group.

The player laughed. "We know who y'all are! You're the talk of the town!" He motioned to the ballists beside him. "We're the New Orleans Pelicans, least what remains of us."

"You only have six players in your club?" Graham asked.

"Don't you worry, son." The ballist laughed again. "We'll have plenty of players for the match."

"But only a handful of Pelicans will be playin' for the Pelicans," noted a second ballist.

"Permit me to explain," a third member of the local club chimed in. "The Pelicans used to be the team to beat in these parts, and Fred Abbott over here used to be our backstop." He motioned with his cap to the ballist who had spoken first. "I'm Abner Powell. I used to pitch for the Pelicans. Used to manage 'em, too. I'll be steering the ship once again this weekend."

"Why do you say 'used to'?" Griffith asked. "You all have uniforms. Don't you play anymore?"

**BACKSTOP:** *catcher.*

"Back in ninety-six, we were the champs of the Southern League," the second ballist spoke again. "The name's Frenchy Genins, and I played center scout for that pennant-winning club. This here's Joe Stanley. He patrolled left garden." He motioned with his thumb to the ballist beside him. "But after our championship run, the league had money woes and had to shut its doors."

"Most of our ballists have gone their

235

separate ways," Abner Powell spoke up again. "Lucien Smith was my ace hurler on that ninety-six squad, and what I wouldn't pay to see him take the hill one more time!" The Pelicans' manager shrugged. "But he needs to earn a living. He's got a lot of mouths to feed up there in Slidell."

"But don't you worry," Joe Stanley said, pointing to Griffith. "Mr. Powell's assembled quite the team for this weekend. Bunch of college boys from Tulane are going to be playing with us."

"Speaking of playing," said Abner Powell, "would you mind letting us take the field with you?"

"We would be honored," Professor Lance replied.

Moments later, the New Orleans Pelicans and the Travelin' Nine were practicing side by side on the green oasis. The barnstormers even displayed some Southern hospitality of their own. Scribe, who was about to bat, allowed the local ballists to jump in front and take some cuts. Crazy Feet in left and Guy behind the dish both stepped aside so the hometowners could get in some work. And Preacher Wil yielded the mound to the Pelican hurler so that he could throw batting practice to his teammates.

Ruby, Happy, and Owen continued to keep a close watch on their surroundings. Griffith and Graham, on the other hand, couldn't take their eyes off the field. Graham imitated what was taking place on the pitch, swinging along with the strikers and pretending to make catches like the scouts in the outer garden. Griffith scouted the opposing players and made mental notes for the skills competition on Friday and the match on Saturday.

**SCOUT (v.):** *to observe and evaluate players on the opposing side.*

"You kids want to play some?" Powell asked after taking his batting practice swings.

"Oh, yeah!" Graham exclaimed.

237

But before Graham could take him up on the offer, Ruby burst out of nowhere and bolted by *both* her brothers. Dashing to the dish, she took the lumber right out of Abner Powell's hands!

As Ruby stepped to the plate, her brothers took the field. Graham raced out toward second sack, while Griffith positioned himself between Scribe, Woody, and Frenchy Genins in right center. And Abner Powell jogged back to the hill.

*Sluggers*

Propping the bat on her shoulder, Ruby rubbed the baseball in her pocket for luck, then ran her fingers along the chain of keys she now wore around her neck.

"See if you can reach me, sis!" Graham called.

Ruby took Powell's first pitch.

"What are you doing?" shouted Graham. "You swing at everything close during batting practice. We don't have all—"

*Crack!*

Ruby laced a liner in Graham's direction. The smash came so fast he had little time to react. He leaped for the rising rope, but it was already beyond his fingertips. The ball was hit so hard, it even found a hole between Griffith and the three other ballists in the outer garden.

"What are you doing?" Ruby mocked. "You're supposed to catch everything close during fielding practice. We don't have all—"

**LINER:**
*line-drive batted ball.*

**ROPE:**
*hard throw or batted ball.*

**240**

"I almost had that!" Graham cut her off, swatting his leather against his leg.

Ruby pointed the timber at her brother. "Almost doesn't count in this game!"

# 17

★

## Fliers and Fans
## in the French Quarter

**uby counted the remain-**ing fliers in her hand. In a few minutes, she would need to return to the satchel—for the *fifth* time—to retrieve yet another stack.

"Everyone's heard of you guys!" she said to Doc, Woody, and Crazy Feet, the three ballists accompanying her as she spread the word about the baseball festival.

"I reckon it's a little overwhelming being well known," Woody said.

"A little?" replied Doc. "Try a lot overwhelming!"

Since the Travelin' Nine had headed straight from practice to the French Quarter, the players were still in uniform. Without question, that helped them stand out, but even if the ballists hadn't been wearing their game attire, Ruby believed many of the passersby would have still recognized these Rough Riders.

"Here you go, sir," she said, passing a flier to a man. "And here you go too." She handed one to the boy by his side.

"If the weather cooperates," Woody said, "I reckon we're going to make ourselves a pretty penny this weekend."

"It seems like everyone Ruby greets is going to the skills competition or the match," Doc added.

"Or both!" declared Woody.

Ruby stepped to a woman holding a parasol. "Here you go, ma'am," she said, passing her the last flier.

The woman tapped the paper. "I can't

wait to see the Pelicans take the field again," she said. "Those boys deserve to be playing ball. It's a shame their team's folded these last couple seasons."

"Time for my next batch!" Ruby announced. She brushed her hands as if she had just completed a hearty meal.

With the three ballists tailing close behind, Ruby headed over to Uncle Owen and Happy, sitting with the satchel of fliers on a bench by the entranceway to Jackson Square.

Unlike back in St. Louis, Elizabeth allowed the Travelin' Nine and her children to break into smaller groups. However, once again, she insisted they take extra precautions. For one thing, Uncle Owen and Happy had to sit by the gate in front of St. Louis Cathedral and serve as lookouts. If anyone suspicious-looking entered the square, they were to alert the others with a series of whistles. In addition, Griffith, Ruby, and Graham were each assigned *three* adults to stay with them at all times. Scribe, Elizabeth, and Tales shadowed Graham, while the Professor, Bubbles, Preacher Wil, and Truman accompanied Griffith.

Unfortunately, Griffith wasn't having nearly as much success with the fliers as his sister. He was far too distracted and nervous, even with all the additional precautionary measures. He didn't like it that the Chancellor and his goons had yet to show themselves in New Orleans. They were up to something.

Griffith lowered his eyes to Truman, and once more, that uneasy feeling settled in his stomach. Why did he so often feel frightened when he looked Truman's way?

# BASEBALL FESTIVAL
## EXTRAVAGANZA ☞

Two Fun-Filled, Action-Packed Days

Friday, September 1 and Saturday, September 2, 1899

On the Grounds of Crescent City Base Ball Park in Mid-City

# TRAVELIN' NINE

vs.

# NEW ORLEANS PELICANS

## Friday, September 1

# SKILLS COMPETITION

**Dead-Eye Accuracy Throw**

**Golden Arm Longest Throw**

**Home-to-Home Speed Contest**

**Soft Hands Juggling Contest**

**Heavy Lumber Longest Strike**

## FIRST EVENT
## 10:00 A.M.

Admission

## 5 Cents

## Saturday, September 2

# BASEBALL MATCH

## Hometown New Orleans Pelicans

vs.

## World Famous Travelin' Nine

## FIRST PITCH
## 2:00 P.M.

Admission

## 25 cents
for adults

## 10 cents
for children

# 18

★

## Someone Is Someone Else

"M y cousins are visionaries," Bubbles declared. He stood at the end of the long, rectangular dinner table with his glass raised high. "You mock me today, but—"

"We mock you every day!" Doc interrupted.

All the barnstormers seated around the table laughed.

"Eight days a week!" added the Professor.

The ballists roared.

"Laugh all you want," Bubbles said, stroking what remained of his left ear and then pointing at his teammates. "One day you'll be telling your grandkids how old Bubbles was the one who let you in on the secret of that first flying machine the brothers Wright built up in Dayton."

"We sure will," Tales put in. "We'll tell our grandkids that's what old Bubbles was shouting about as they carted him off to the funny farm!"

The room erupted.

Of course, the dinner-table ribbing was all in good fun. And even though the Rough Riders were raucous, their antics weren't disturbing any of the other restaurant patrons.

Thanks to Happy.

After the barnstormers finished passing out the fliers, the team decided to head to Happy's favorite restaurant and tavern, located on nearby Bourbon Street. The manager on duty at Lafitte's Blacksmith Shop recognized Happy the moment he stepped through the door, and because it was still early, he was able to allow the three Payne kids and Truman into the establishment. On top of that, he gave the group a back room away from all the other diners.

Because they had the private area all to themselves, Griffith could breathe a little easier and enjoy the meal. And what a meal it was! The barnstormers sampled and savored a variety of tasty and *spicy* foods. Griffith and Ruby loved the jambalaya, filled with chicken, sausage, rice, and vegetables, while Graham's favorite dish was the soup-like gumbo.

"It reminds me of the burgoo we had in Louisville," Graham said. "Only this tastes a million times better."

Ruby covered her smile and leaned into Griffith. "Don't tell him they're almost identical," she whispered, "except for the name."

For dessert, the team feasted on beignets, deep-fried pastries smothered in confectioner's sugar. Not surprisingly, more of the white powder ended up on Graham's face than in his mouth. In addition, as Bubbles was telling his tall tales, the manager walked in with a tray full of pralines, candylike cookies made with pecans and—

Suddenly the room fell silent. Several members of the Pelicans—Joe Stanley, Abner Powell, and one who hadn't been at practice—slowly entered. Each ballist seemed more nervous and on edge than the next.

Seconds later it was clear why. Two of the Chancellor's thugs, wearing their trademark dark suits, pink pocket squares, and hats, followed the hometowners in.

As soon as they appeared, Scribe sprang from his seat, leaped in front of Graham—who was two chairs the door—and folded his arms across his chest. Woody stood up too and sped over to Griffith and Ruby, sitting next to each other on the far side of the table. Bubbles, who was standing near to the doorway, was now shoulder to shoulder with one of the goons. He clenched his fists and gritted his teeth. And Truman, lying under the table, began to growl.

"We are . . . we are not able to compete against you this weekend," Abner Powell stammered. "The festival . . . the festival has been canceled."

"Why?" The Professor pounded the table.

Powell swallowed. "Because . . . because one of the Travelin' Nine isn't who he says he is."

Griffith gasped. He locked eyes with the thug closest to Joe Stanley. It was the goon from the train who'd taken the ball from Ruby. Griffith's chest tightened.

"What does that mean?" the Professor barked. "Who isn't—what does that mean?"

"Let me put it to you this way," replied Joe Stanley, glancing to the goon by his side. "One of your players isn't who *she* says she is."

The thug from the train raised his arm and pointed to Elizabeth, who was sitting at the far end of the table by Happy and Owen.

"Take off your hat," Joe Stanley said.

Without hesitation, Elizabeth rose from her chair, removed her cap, and shook out her hair. "I am exactly who I say I am," she said defiantly.

"You are a woman disguised as a man," said Joe Stanley, stepping forward. "You have—you have committed a fraud against—defrauded this team and our city." He stumbled over his own words like an actor who had forgotten his lines. "The festival is no more."

"This has got to stop!" Ruby shrieked, jumping to her feet.

All the barnstormers faced her.

"Ruby, please," said Elizabeth, reaching across the table for her daughter.

"No!" Ruby shouted. But her angry answer wasn't aimed at her mother. Nor was it aimed at the Pelicans or even the Chancellor's men. It was directed at the Rough Riders. "How can you do this to us?"

Now Griffith rose from his seat. He pivoted to his sister and placed his hands on her shaking shoulders. Slowly, and without saying a word, he eased her back into her chair.

But then Bubbles erupted.

"No!" he shouted. "Ruby's right. This has got to stop!"

Suddenly Bubbles leaped onto the table. Glasses toppled, dishes broke, and silverware sailed.

Everyone ducked for cover. None of the barnstormers had ever seen this wild side of Bubbles before. Not even on the battlefield in Cuba.

"Elizabeth Payne *will* play in the baseball festival this weekend," he declared, stomping his boot on the table. He pointed at the thugs. "This festival *will* go on."

"The decision has already been made," Joe Stanley said.

"Decision overruled!" Bubbles fired back.

"Get down, Bubbles," pleaded Ruby.

Joe Stanley shook his head. "Some of the ballists refuse to take the pitch if—"

"I said, decision overruled!" Bubbles silenced him again.

The Travelin' Nine's shortstop stormed back down the table, and when he reached the end, he lunged for the thugs. But at the last possible instant, Scribe plucked Bubbles out of the air.

"Easy, solider," said Scribe, restraining his teammate. "It's not worth it. Easy."

*Woof!*

Truman barked.

It was only the second time any of the barnstormers had heard the hound bark, and like that first occasion on the train from Minneapolis, it was a bark that meant business.

"Easy, boy," Griffith said, holding back the hound and copying the approach Scribe had taken with Bubbles. "It's not worth it."

"Who is sabotaging what we're trying to achieve?" Bubbles addressed his teammates as Scribe gradually let him go. "Which one of you is it?"

No one uttered a word.

"Which one?" he asked. He began to circle the table. "Which one of you has no honor?" His voice cracked, and tears fell from both eyes. "Which one of you is working for *him*?"

The Rough Riders stayed silent.

Ruby looked to her older brother. They locked eyes, and as soon as they did, Ruby knew exactly what he was thinking. The list of suspects was down to six. Bubbles wasn't the mole.

Griffith stared across the room at the Pelican players. A part of him felt bad for the ballists. There was no doubt in his mind the Chancellor had painted them into an impossible corner. But Griffith also knew he couldn't remain a spectator. He had stayed silent for long enough.

"What's happening here doesn't make any sense," he finally spoke. "I know a thing or two about the Pelicans and about you, Mr. Powell." Griffith stood up to address the team's manager. "I read the plaque by the entrance to Crescent City Ball Park. A few years ago you invented Ladies Day."

Abner Powell swallowed, but did not answer.

"That's right," Griffith went on, nodding. "You created a day where women could attend a match free of charge. You have great respect for women."

Abner Powell lowered his head.

Griffith nodded again. He was certain the Pelicans manager had received his message. He'd wanted Abner Powell to know that he—and all the barnstormers—knew what was *really* happening here.

"You're afraid," Ruby said, rising out of her seat again and pointing to the Chancellor's men. "You're afraid she's better than anyone they'd choose to participate in the festival."

The two thugs laughed.

Ruby pushed in her chair. "You're afraid my mother could take on all the Pelicans and win the skills competition by herself." She walked around the table toward the goons. "You're afraid of a woman."

Griffith covered his smile. Would they take the bait?

"We're not—we're not afraid of anyone,"

Abner Powell said, glancing to the thug on his left.

"Maybe you're not, but *they* are." Ruby snickered. She waved the back of her hand at the Chancellor's men. "They're afraid a woman can throw the pill more accurately and smack the rock farther than any man in the state of Louisiana."

Both thugs shook their heads.

"Ruby, stop," said Elizabeth.

"She can run faster too," Graham chimed in, peeking out from behind Scribe. "And she has a better glove."

"All you can do is stand there and shake your heads." Ruby refused to relent. "Because you know the truth. You know—"

"Children, please," Elizabeth interrupted. "You're not helping the situation. You're not—"

"No!" the thug from the train shouted. It was the first word either of the Chancellor's men had spoken. He motioned to Ruby. "Let the girl speak."

Ruby swallowed. She glanced back to Griffith as if to assure him she had the situation under control.

"Here's how you can prove you're not scared of a woman," she said. "The skills competition still takes place on Friday. My mother will represent the Travelin' Nine. If she wins three of the five events, Saturday's match is back on."

The thug shook his head. "She must win all five events," he responded, holding up his hand with his fingers spread wide.

"If she wins all five, the match takes place?" Ruby asked.

"There will be no match," the thug replied. "There's no way any woman or man could win all five events. Your proposal is so laughable we don't even have to consult with the Chancellor before agreeing to it. He would find it just as amusing and far-fetched as we do." He sneered. "She won't win."

Ruby looked at her mother and then back at the thugs. "We'll see about that."

# 19
## Another Arrives

ll five events?" Elizabeth said to Ruby. "Three out of five is one thing, but this arrangement leaves no margin for error."

"I know you can do it, Mom," Ruby replied confidently. Then she added, "It's not like we have a choice."

Since leaving the restaurant, Ruby hadn't left her mother's side. As they walked to the streetcar that ran along St. Charles Avenue,

Ruby repeatedly assured her she had what it took to sweep the skills competition.

Once they boarded, Ruby had hoped Griffith, Graham, or some of the others would echo her words of encouragement. However, everyone was far too enthralled by the streetcar, because it was their first time riding one powered by electricity, and it was their first time riding one at night.

After disembarking, Ruby insisted that she and her mother walk in front of the group. Ruby wanted her mother to lead them the remaining few blocks back to Happy's, just like she was going to lead them to victory on Friday.

Suddenly Elizabeth stopped dead in her tracks.

"My word," she whispered.

Ruby froze. Josiah sat on Happy's front-porch swing. Even through the darkness, she could see his unmistakable form.

Josiah rose from his seat, and the eagle, who'd been perched on the back of the porch swing, spread its majestic wings and hopped onto the railing.

Ruby glanced back at the others. The barnstormers stood in a silent row.

Moving slowly, Josiah walked down the stairs and up the front path to Graham. "It's good to see you again, Mr. Graham," he said, smiling.

"It's good to see you again too," Graham replied.

"You've grown quite a bit since I first laid eyes on you."

Graham scrunched his face into a knot. "The trolley was just last week. And Minneapolis was less—"

Josiah held up his hand. "I carried you home." He shuffled over to Elizabeth and placed a hand over his chest. "I am sorry for your loss, Mrs. Elizabeth."

"My word," she whispered.

She swallowed. "Thank you."

"You have a beautiful family."

"Thank you," Elizabeth repeated. "You look exactly the same."

"I'm not so sure that's a good thing." He reached out, rested a hand on her shoulder, and peered at her with his different-colored eyes. "Harm will not come to your family, Mrs. Elizabeth. I promise."

"Thank you," she uttered for a third time.

He faced the Travelin' Nine. "I have much to discuss with everyone," he said. "It's been a long few days of travel. Would it be possible—"

"Say no more," Happy interrupted. "We insist you stay here with us."

"Thank you, Mr. Happy." Josiah bowed. "I was hoping you would say that." He then peered down at Truman, who had sat beside him. He scratched behind the dog's floppy ears and teased the fur in the white spots on his back.

"His name's Truman," Griffith said quietly. Earlier, when Josiah had first seen Truman, Griffith had thought he'd detected an expression of surprise on his face, almost as if the old man was *stunned* to see that Truman was still alive and well.

Griffith had no idea what to make of this.

"Permit me to bring the little that I have inside," said Josiah. "Then we must talk."

# 20

★

## A Great Burden

arlier this week," Josiah began, his voice somber, "I saw my son for the first time in years." He peered around the room at the barnstormers. "He's no longer the boy or young man I once knew. He looks like a man twice his age. Hatred does that to a body."

Griffith turned his head. As much as he wanted to look at Josiah as he spoke, he couldn't. The old man's expression was too pained.

When Uncle Owen had addressed the group, the meeting had taken place in the large living area. But this evening the team convened in a different room, also located on the ground floor, but toward the back of the house. It was a room Happy rarely unlocked, but he'd decided to open it for this special occasion.

Everyone was here except Owen. He didn't have the strength to attend the meeting. In fact, right after Griffith and Woody had helped him to his room, Owen had fallen asleep.

As soon as Happy had opened the door, the Rough Riders understood why it was a special place. The room contained a striking collection of military artifacts and souvenirs. Happy's neatly pressed uniform hung on a wooden hanger on the outside of a closet door. Corps badges—some clover-shaped, a few resembling stars, and one that looked like a buzz saw with nine teeth—were displayed in a museum-like case underneath the three rectangular windows. A pair of dog tags, both with carved and decorative edges, hung from a post affixed to the top of a dresser. On the sofa, the flag of the First United States Volunteer Cavalry was draped across an armrest. In the canton, an eagle, which appeared to be in flight, held the "*e pluribus unum*" ribbon in its mouth, sticks in one set of talons and branches in the other.

Josiah sat on the wooden trunk in which Happy had carefully placed the flag so that the three Payne children and Elizabeth could all sit on the sofa.

"My worst nightmare has become a reality," the old man began, clasping his hands in his lap. "My only son has turned into something far worse than I'd ever imagined."

Griffith shut his eyes. Then he reached

down and stroked Truman's neck and back. The sleeping hound lay across his feet.

"I am deeply troubled," Josiah went on, "for I fear there is no longer any good left in my son. I know a father should always believe in his . . ." Josiah stopped and ran his fingers along the deep creases of his forehead. "But I do believe we can defeat him. So long as we are one. We must be, in order to confront . . . such a sinister force."

"Josiah," said Griffith, raising his hand like he would in school, "I've already told them everything you shared with me back in Minneapolis."

"Thank you, Mr. Griffith. That is good to know." Josiah stood up and walked to the center of the room. "My son covets two things: the baseball and Mr. Graham. If he ever gains possession of that which he seeks, the power he will possess . . ." Josiah did not finish this thought either. He stepped to

"The Chancellor envies . . . you."

Graham. "Mr. Graham, these next words I say to you."

Griffith peered around his mother at Graham. His brother held Ruby's hand, the one that wasn't in her pocket on the baseball.

"Mr. Graham, you are the chosen one. The very future of the great game of baseball rests with you. I know that's a tremendous weight for a boy to carry. It's a great burden for any man, but you must know what you are up against. What *we* are up against."

Graham nodded. Josiah's words didn't frighten him. Perhaps they should have, but instead they filled him with confidence.

"The Chancellor envies and resents you for having the future he once believed belonged to him," Josiah continued. He placed a hand on Graham's shoulder. "The Chancellor knows he cannot rule the game of baseball by playing it. However, he believes he can rule the game with *you* playing it."

Graham let go of his sister's hand, stood

up, and looked deep into Josiah's eyes. "I won't let him."

"Mr. Graham, he will rig the outcome of matches, cause injury to players, and alter rules to fit his aims. He will assemble a team of ballists centered around you. This team will be dominant and all-powerful." Josiah nodded. "Power. Corruption. Greed. Do not allow yourself to think for one moment he cannot achieve these objectives."

"I won't let him," Graham repeated.

"None of us are going to, Mr. Graham." Josiah nodded again and then looked to Elizabeth. "You will win the skills competition."

"That's what I've been telling her," said Ruby, tightening her grip on the baseball in her pocket.

Josiah peered out the trio of rectangular windows at the eagle sitting up tall on the lateral limb of a live oak. "We will not let you lose."

# 21

★

## *Skills and Thrills*

ou ready, Mom?" Ruby asked.

"Ready as I'll ever be," Elizabeth replied as she prepared to step onto the field for the Dead-Eye Accuracy Throw, the first event of the skills competition.

"Take it one event at a time," advised Ruby.

"One event? Try one *throw* at a time!" Elizabeth kissed the top of Ruby's head. "Go keep your brothers company." She nodded to Griffith and Graham, who stood with the ballists behind the first bag line.

Then Elizabeth started juggling again, as she had been all morning. She wasn't juggling to practice for the Soft Hands Juggling Contest taking place later. Nor was she trying to show off. Elizabeth juggled because it helped her stay focused and remain relaxed.

As Ruby headed back to the others, she gazed about at the hundreds of cranks who'd descended on the practice fields adjacent to Crescent City Base Ball Park. Even though it was barely ten in the morning, the spectators were already standing three and four deep. By the main tent area, on the far side of the temporary fence erected behind the fields, the line to purchase tickets stretched out the tent and a third of the way around the stadium.

The beautiful weather certainly played a role in the large turnout. Not only had the skies cleared, but the oppressive humidity had abated as well. Sure it was still plenty hot, but by late summer, the citizens of New Orleans were used to temperatures in the nineties.

The dry heat also improved the playing conditions on the field. While the pitch was still damp, all the standing water was gone. Even the large puddle next to the mound where Truman had taken up residence during batting practice had evaporated.

Working her way through the onlookers, Ruby could feel the excitement. Many of the cranks were just getting word that today's skills competition between the Pelicans and the Travelin' Nine had turned into a battle of the sexes. Ruby sensed that some of the women in the crowd were secretly (and not so secretly) pulling for her mother.

"How's Mom doing?" Griffith asked when she reached the sidelines.

The Rough Riders, standing directly behind the Payne boys, leaned in.

"She's nervous," Ruby replied, "but she's up to the challenge."

"She'll be fine," Graham stated confidently. "She just needs to make her first throw."

Griffith smiled at his brother. "Since when did you become the voice of reason?" he asked.

Graham was right. All the buildup and anticipation would make anyone anxious. But once the events got underway, Elizabeth Payne would be just fine. Griffith was as certain as Graham (maybe even more so).

Standing on his toes, Griffith peered around at the cranks. He was sure about something else, too. It was only a matter of time until the Chancellor and his men tried something.

"Mr. Griffith," Josiah said, stepping in front of him, "let me worry about the Chancellor." He reached out and tapped the boy's temple. "I see that's what concerns you.

You cannot let it today." He lifted his fingers from the side of Griffith's head and pointed to the eagle perched high atop the roof of the ballpark. "Mr. Griffith, concentrate solely on your mother. She will win. I promise."

In the Dead-Eye Accuracy Throw, the contestants were each given three balls. From the catcher's position behind home dish, they aimed for a target—a hollowed-out wheel mounted to the top of a piece of plywood— just beyond second sack. A large piece of brown paper with red, white, and blue concentric rings painted on it was draped over the wheel.

The Pelicans' player, a young ballist none of the barnstormers had ever seen before, elected to take his three throws first.

"Who is this kid?" Griffith growled, suspicious of the newcomer. "Is he one of the Chancellor's pawns?"

"I believe he's one of those Tulane boys," the Professor replied.

"I heard he's the star third sack man for the university," added Preacher Wil. "They say he's got quite the cannon."

"So does my mom," said Griffith.

He knew this was her specialty. No one threw the pill from home plate to second sack better than Elizabeth Payne. Not even Guy Payne himself. Griffith was relieved this was the first event of the skills competition.

**CANNON:** *strong throwing arm.*

But for right now, she had to wait her turn.

As the hometown ballist stepped to the mark, the cranks cheered loudly. He tipped his cap to his supporters and then fired his first throw.

*Pop!*

The first pill penetrated the outer red circle. The crowd roared.

But his second throw sailed harmlessly into center garden. The crowd groaned.

The ballist blew on his hand several times before grabbing the rock for his final throw.

*Pop!*

The ball blasted through part of the white circle and part of the bull's-eye blue circle. The crowd erupted again.

"Beat that," he muttered to Elizabeth, brushing by her on his way back to his teammates.

The Travelin' Nine and the three Paynes all heard the Pelican player, but Elizabeth didn't so much as break stride or look in his direction. With her game face on, she headed straight for the thrower's mark.

"Go, Mom!" Graham cheered with his hands cupped around his mouth.

Ruby gazed around at the cranks. They had no idea that Elizabeth *had* to win this event. If she lost the Dead-Eye Accuracy Throw, tomorrow's match would be canceled. The fans would be furious.

But her mother was going to win. Ruby refused to allow herself to harbor any doubts. She squeezed the baseball in her pocket.

Out on the field, Elizabeth stepped to the mark. She stared down at the fresh target draped over the wagon wheel behind second base and windmilled her arm like Happy so often did when he used to toe the rubber for the Travelin' Nine. Then Elizabeth removed her cap and shook out her hair, as if to remind all in attendance that a woman was about to unleash these throws.

**RUBBER:** *pitching strip on the mound. The pitcher must have one foot touching the rubber when pitching.*

Not that anyone needed reminding.

Suddenly Elizabeth picked her catcher's mitt off the ground and crouched behind the dish.

"What's Mom doing?" asked Graham. "She doesn't need her glove."

"I know exactly what she's doing," Griffith replied.

"So do I!" Ruby declared. "Mom throws best after catching a pitch. She's pretending it's a real game!"

Elizabeth pounded her mitt twice, leaped out of her squat, and fired her first throw.

*Pop!*

The pill pierced the blue center of the target!

"Bull's-eye!" all three Paynes and many of the Rough Riders shouted as one.

"She did it!" shouted Graham. "Mom won!"

"Not yet," Ruby corrected him. "She still has to hit the target with one of her next two throws."

"Like I said," Graham announced, raising his fists triumphantly, "she won!"

Griffith placed a hand on his brother's shoulder. "Don't count your—"

*Whoosh!*

Elizabeth uncorked her second throw, and

Elizabeth . . . fired her first throw.

like the first one, it headed straight for the center of the target. The ball passed *through* the wheel, but there was still only *one* hole in the middle blue circle.

"What happened?" Doc asked.

"Where did it go?" Woody wondered.

"I'll tell you where," said Graham, raising his fists again. "Mom's second throw went right through the first hole! I was right. She won!"

Indeed she had. Elizabeth needed only two throws to win the Dead-Eye Accuracy Throw.

"Huzzah!" Tales and the Professor cheered as Elizabeth returned to her teammates and family.

"Job well done, Mrs. Elizabeth," Josiah said, shaking her hand. "That was quite a show you put on."

As everyone offered their congratulations, Ruby noticed that some of the *women* cranks were also cheering for her mother . . . even as the men standing nearby shot them looks of disgust.

"Thank you, everyone," Elizabeth said, holding up her hands. "But that was only the first event. There are four more left."

"One down, four to go!" Griffith declared.

Even though Elizabeth had won the first competition, she wasn't offered the choice of whether she preferred to go first or second for the next event, the Golden Arm Longest Throw. Once again, the same Pelican player opted to lead things off.

For this contest, the participants stood by home dish, just like they had for the Dead-

Eye Accuracy Throw. However, that was where the similarities between the two tests of skill ended. In the Golden Arm Longest Throw, each contestant was allotted only one turn (not three), and they no longer aimed for a fixed target. Instead they threw the rawhide as far as they could toward center garden, where a series of distance markers had been placed on the turf.

"Mom might need a little help with this one," Ruby whispered to Griffith.

"I was thinking the same thing," he said.

While Elizabeth Payne had the most accurate arm on the Travelin' Nine, she didn't have the strongest. That honor belonged to Woody. That wasn't to say Elizabeth didn't have a riflelike arm. She most certainly did. It just didn't compare to the right scout's.

Ruby lifted the baseball from her pocket and waved for Graham.

As soon as he took his first step toward

his brother and sister, Scribe's heavy hand landed on the littlest Payne's shoulder. Graham wasn't going anywhere without Scribe at his side.

"I have my own personal shade tree today," Graham joked. He motioned to Scribe's enormous shadow, which shielded him from the sun.

"A tree offers shelter and protection," said Scribe, nodding. "That is what I'm providing."

Ruby held the baseball out to her brothers and waited for them to place their hands on it. She peeked up at Scribe. With their baseball out in the open, she was happy to have the hulking center scout hovering over them. Then she turned toward the dish.

The cranks cheered as the Pelican player stepped to the thrower's mark and raised the rock high over his head. Then he looked to Elizabeth (who was juggling again) and began windmilling his arm, just like she had prior to the previous event. He took a giant crow hop and fired the ball.

*Whoosh!*

The hometowner's throw soared toward center garden and didn't land until it reached the second-to-last marker near the edge of the outfield.

The cranks erupted. Their hoots and whistles echoed off the stadium's facade.

"You can't beat that!" shouted one.

"No woman can even *think* about throwing a ball that far!" yelled another.

"*Lady* luck has run out!" hollered a third.

As she headed for the thrower's mark, Elizabeth continued to juggle. Not once did she break stride or even so much as glance in the direction of the cranks.

Ruby looked to her brothers and then back at the three hands resting atop the baseball.

On the field, Elizabeth had finally stopped

**CROW HOP:** *fielding technique a player uses in order to provide balance and throwing momentum after a catch.*

juggling and was now windmilling her arm as she prepared to make her throw. She picked up her mitt, stepped behind the dish, and again crouched into a catcher's position. Then she popped up like a spring and fired.

*Whoosh!*

The baseball flew out of her hand, rising over the pitcher's mound and sailing past second sack. But above the outer garden, the ball began losing speed, and in an instant, Griffith, Ruby, and Graham all realized their mother's throw was going to come up short.

"Go, ball!" Graham pleaded.

"More, more, more!" urged Griffith.

Ruby opened her mouth to cheer, but words wouldn't follow. She inhaled a deep breath, hoping the additional air would help. When it didn't, she exhaled a long puff, *blowing* on the three hands and the baseball.

Suddenly Elizabeth's throw started to

gain height and speed. It had caught a second wind! Riding that tailwind, the ball soared way beyond the final distance marker in center garden. It didn't return to earth until it reached the onlookers gathered behind the last rope in the farthest spot from home plate.

"Mom wins!" Graham exclaimed. "Two for two!"

Elizabeth charged back to the sidelines, and once again the barnstormers greeted her with handshakes, hugs, and huzzahs. A growing number of cranks—no longer just women—applauded her achievement too. While they may not have been rooting for her, they surely appreciated what she had accomplished.

"Did we do that?" Ruby said to Griffith as the others continued to celebrate.

"We?" he replied. "You were the one who blew on the baseball. You were—"

# 22

★

## The Elizabeth Payne Show

**he cranks who spotted the** well-dressed posse in back of the spectators in right garden didn't know what to make of them. Some squinted for a closer look, some scratched their heads, and some traded questioning glances. But one thing was clear: The thugs respected, or perhaps feared, the man with the cobralike face who issued commands with a wave of the hand or a stare.

Once the similarly dressed men finished setting up a small, roped-off area behind the onlookers, a pair trudged through the crowd, which parted like a biblical sea, toward the Pelican players. Mothers reached for their children and husbands drew their wives closer as the dark-suited duo passed.

When the twosome reached the hometown ballists, they cornered Abner Powell. While most couldn't hear the exchange, it was apparent to all that the news they delivered was chilling, for moments later the Pelican player who had lost the two throwing contests was escorted from the field by several teammates.

"I reckon we won't be seein' him again," said Woody, frowning.

Scribe placed both of his oversize hands on Graham's shoulders. "You stay directly in front of me at all times," he said to the youngest Payne. "You're not to be out of my sight or out of my reach."

"Yes, sir," Graham replied.

Griffith was about to offer a few additional

words of caution when, out of the corner of his eye, he spotted Josiah sneaking off. Down the right garden line, the old man ducked behind a group of parasol-toting women and disappeared into the crowd. He didn't want his son to see him.

Turning back toward the field, Griffith gazed in amazement at the number of spectators now in attendance. All along the perimeter of the pitch, more and more cranks were appearing by the minute. There had to be well over a thousand onlookers on hand. Maybe even two thousand. Griffith performed some quick calculations in his head. If the number of fans continued to grow, and if his mother won the competition, the barnstormers would easily raise $150 today!

**DIAMOND:** *infield.*

But Griffith was getting *way* ahead of himself. So far she'd won only two events. She needed to win three more.

Across the diamond, the two thugs

continued to speak with Abner Powell. One of the goons motioned to a Pelican player, and the other pointed in the direction of the Chancellor. Then they headed back through the crowd. By the time they rejoined their crew, the hometown ballist they had hand-picked was stepping onto the field for the Home-to-Home Speed Contest.

The player bolted to home plate.

Elizabeth looked to Crazy Feet. "Any final words of wisdom?"

The fastest ballist on the barnstormers tapped his temple and smiled.

Elizabeth pumped her fists and then charged to the dish.

"What do you think that meant?" Graham asked his sister.

"It means if she runs a smart race, she's going to win."

"That's what I thought," said Graham, nodding. "Just checking."

The Home-to-Home Speed Contest was identical to the dash around the diamond held prior to the game way back in Louisville. Crazy Feet had lost that contest, though most of the Rough Riders blamed his defeat on the fact that he had to run the bases in the reverse direction.

Just like Elizabeth. Upon reaching home plate, that was the direction she was assigned to run.

"Let's all hold the baseball again," Graham said.

Once more, the three Paynes joined hands on the ball.

"Would you like for me to call the race?" Tales asked, stepping forward.

Bubbles chuckled. "Do we have a choice?"

"You don't have to listen," said Tales, playfully pushing his teammate aside. "Everyone else can enjoy my play-by-play!" He faced the field, put his hands on his knees, and waited for the runners to break from the line.

Griffith sized up the contestants and smiled. While his mother appeared as calm and composed as ever, the Pelican player seemed a bit *jumpy*. He anxiously shook out his arms and hands, and every few seconds he glanced toward the area behind the cranks down the right garden line.

"*Go!*" the umpire called.

"And they're off!" Tales announced. "The Pelican flies into the early lead. He reaches first bag a stride before Elizabeth Payne reaches third. But here comes the barnstormers' backstop. As she passes the shortstop area, she has closed the gap. Both racers cross second simultaneously. But the Pelican makes a wide turn and drifts toward the outfield grass. A terrible error by the local product! Elizabeth Payne takes the lead! She crosses first sack a full two steps before the Pelican lands on third."

"You can do it, Mom!" Ruby shouted, squeezing her brothers' fingers atop the baseball.

"As the two runners head for home," cried Tales, "the Pelican player is catching up! But did he wait too long to make his move? Who's it going to be?" Tales hopped into the air. "Elizabeth Payne crosses the plate first and wins!"

"Three for three!" Graham cheered, leaping even higher than Tales.

He broke for the field, but before he managed to take a single step, Scribe grabbed him by the back of his collar and pulled him back in.

"Great job, Mom," Ruby greeted her mother, who didn't break stride until she was next to her family and teammates.

"I reckon you ran a better race than Crazy Feet!" Woody declared.

*Sluggers*

Griffith turned to thank the Travelin' Nine's left scout for advising and supporting his mother, but somewhat surprisingly, he didn't see him. Focusing on the crowd instead, he couldn't believe his eyes and ears. Most of the cranks—women *and* men—were now cheering for his mother. Even the fans standing near the Chancellor's crew were rooting for Elizabeth Payne.

"Sweep! Sweep!" chanted a group of onlookers behind home plate.

Griffith knew his mother wasn't thinking about sweeping all five events. She was taking the skills competition one event at a time, and right now, she had to focus on the Soft Hands Juggling Contest.

Back across the pitch, the two thugs were once again alongside the Pelican ballists. One had a finger in Abner Powell's face and the other paced in front of the players. Griffith watched as Joe Stanley handed a set

300

of baseballs to a teammate, who then headed for home plate, where Elizabeth was already warming up.

For this event, the two contestants stood on opposite sides of the plate facing each other. When the umpire lowered his arm, they would start to juggle three balls apiece. The first player to drop a ball would be eliminated, and the other would be declared the winner of the duel.

"Let's go, Mom!" Ruby cheered.

"Stay focused," called Happy.

The umpire raised one hand high overhead

and motioned with his other for the contestants to get set.

*"Go!"*

On the umpire's call, both ballists began.
The cranks clapped and cheered, keeping
rhythm with the flight and rotation of the
balls. For the first few minutes, the two sets of
baseballs appeared to be perfectly in sync.

But then the Pelican player began to *tease*
Elizabeth. First he stuck out his tongue.
Then he bobbed his head and rolled his
neck. Finally he made funny faces. However,
Elizabeth kept her eyes on the balls.

So the hometown ballist attempted to
*intimidate* Elizabeth by showing off. He
juggled extra fast. Then he alternated the
rotation of his throws. He mixed in behind-
the-back tosses, followed by under-the-leg
flips. But Elizabeth was unflappable.

Frustrated and fatigued, the Pelican
player started to wobble. His arms shook,

and bullet-size beads began building on his brow. The droplets of perspiration trickled down. He blinked and blinked as the salty sweat blurred his vision. But he blinked one too many times. He lost sight of a base-ball. It deflected off his fingertips and fell to the dirt.

"We have a winner!" declared the umpire. He waited for Elizabeth to stop juggling, then raised her arm.

"Four for four!" Graham exclaimed.

"One more to go!" added Griffith.

"Sweep! Sweep!" a growing number of fans chanted.

Over the din of the roaring rooters, a jubi-lant Elizabeth raced back to the sidelines. Even though she still needed to win one more event, she couldn't hide her excitement. She waved her cap to the cranks.

It all came down to one final test of skills, the Heavy Lumber Longest Strike. And like

**ROOTERS:** *fans; people who cheer at ball games. Also called "cranks" (see page 144).*

everyone else at the practice fields, Elizabeth could see what was taking place on the far side of the pitch.

Yet again, the Chancellor's men approached the Pelicans, but this time there were four of them. They surrounded Abner Powell, who was clearly unnerved by their presence. He lowered his head, pulled his cap down over his eyes, and folded his arms tightly across his chest.

Then, from among the sea of spectators near where the Chancellor and his men congregated, emerged an imposing man. He wasn't nearly as tall and wide as Scribe (who was?), but he was quite sizable nonetheless.

"I don't like the way this looks," Ruby whispered to her brothers.

Griffith ran a hand through his thick hair. Yes, the Chancellor had recruited a ringer for the final event.

"I say we start holding on to the baseball

now," Graham said. "Mom's going to need all the help she can get."

Once again, the three Payne siblings joined hands on their baseball.

Then Griffith peered down the right garden line, and for the first time since the Chancellor's arrival, he was able to spot Josiah. He stood along the rope in the corner, and at the moment he was gesturing to the eagle, who remained high atop the adjacent ballpark. Griffith remembered Josiah's words.

*We will not let you lose.*

Out on the green oasis, Elizabeth had returned to home dish, where she stood face-to-chest with her opponent.

For the Heavy Lumber Longest Strike event, the contestants would each take three swings. They would alternate turns, and the participant who ended up hitting the longest ball would win the contest. The ballists were allowed to select which hurler they wanted to face. The hometowner picked Abner Powell. Elizabeth chose Preacher Wil.

She glanced back at her three children and smiled.

"One more, Mom," Graham called, holding up a single finger.

"You can do it," Ruby said through gritted teeth.

Elizabeth touched her cap and then turned back to her opponent, who was digging in at the dish. The huge human extended his arms and pointed with his lumber where he wanted Abner Powell's pitch to cross the plate.

*Crack!*

The Pelican player blasted his first hit, a titanic shot that soared over the onlookers deep into left-center garden and didn't land until it was twenty or thirty feet *beyond* the last distance marker.

The cranks may have been rooting for Elizabeth, but they couldn't help but show their appreciation for the eye-popping star chaser. Many in the crowd had never seen a ball travel that far.

The Travelin' Nine knew Elizabeth had never hit the rawhide such a distance. How could she possibly win now?

But Elizabeth was unfazed. She strode to the striker's line for her first swing.

Preacher Wil performed some last-minute mound maintenance with his boot and stretched out his arm. Then the south-paw toed the rubber and stared at the spot where Elizabeth wanted the pitch. Finally he rocked into his motion and delivered.

**STRIKER'S LINE:** *batter's box.*

*Crackle!*

Elizabeth popped the pill into the crowd *behind* home plate.

Some in the crowd cheered politely, but it was barely audible over the collective groan.

"The lady's luck has finally run out," quipped one crank.

"All good things must come to an end," added another.

However, Elizabeth remained relaxed, calm, and composed. With her head held high and the same confidence in her step, she walked back over to her teammates.

"Couple more chances," she said, holding up two fingers and smiling.

**MOONSHOT:**
*high fly ball.*

Ruby looked down at the three hands on the baseball and then up at her two brothers. Griffith and Graham couldn't hide their concern either. She chewed her lower lip.

*Crack!*

The Pelican striker launched a second prodigious blast that didn't land until it reached the rooters in the left garden corner. While this next drive may not have traveled nearly the distance as the first moonshot, it still went farther than any ball Elizabeth had ever hit.

"Come on, Mom!" Graham cheered as she headed back to the dish for her second turn. He squeezed his siblings' fingers. "She really needs us," he said.

Ruby gazed out at Preacher Wil preparing to pitch. "I'm going to do what I did for the Golden Arm Longest Throw," she said.

Then Ruby blew hard on the baseball as Preacher Wil released the rock.

*Crackle!*

Elizabeth dribbled a worm burner down to first bag.

The crowd groaned again.

Ruby looked to the Rough Riders. The Professor tugged on the cord of his eye patch. Bubbles held what remained of his left ear. Scribe clasped his huge hands behind his neck. Rarely had she seen the war heroes as worried as they were now.

"Mom," Griffith called, cupping his hand around his mouth. "You're overswinging."

**WORM BURNER:** *ground ball. Also called "ant killer" (see page 85), "bug bruiser" (see page 351), "grass clipper" (see page 355), or "daisy cutter" (see page 381).*

"I'm trying to hit it out of the park," said Elizabeth, nodding.

"Relax your hands," Griffith said. "Open your stance a little. You need to make solid contact."

Elizabeth smiled. "Will do."

Griffith turned around and peered down the right garden line. He searched for Josiah, but the old man was no longer standing along the rope in the corner. Then he turned back toward Crescent City Ball Park. The eagle was gone too. Where did they go? Had something happened to them?

*Crack!*

The hometown striker's third and final hit was another deep drive, this one a hammer to the opposite field. Sailing into the spectators beyond the right-center garden, the rock went nearly as far as his first blast.

"Mom needs us like never before," Griffith said, facing his sister and brother.

**HAMMER:** hard-hit ball. Also known as "stinger" (see page 86).

**OPPOSITE FIELD:** the opposite side of the field from the one to which a batter naturally hits. A right-handed batter's opposite field would be right field; a left-handed batter's would be left field.

"But things aren't working," said Graham.

"They will," said Griffith. He reached down to pet Truman, who was now nestled against his leg, and looked Ruby in the eye. "All positive thoughts and no doubts. There's no tomorrow unless *we* come through."

"Then come through we will!" Graham declared.

"Do you think I should blow on the ball again?" asked Ruby.

"It didn't work for the last swing," Griffith replied, "but it did work earlier when she threw."

"I have an idea," Graham said. "Ruby should blow on the baseball, and we should all point it in the direction we want it to go."

"Excellent!" Griffith exclaimed. "I like that."

Preacher Wil was already rocking into his windup.

Griffith, Ruby, and Graham pointed their

baseball toward the deepest part of left-center garden, and Ruby blew on it as hard as she could. As Preacher Wil's perfectly placed pitch sailed toward the plate, Ruby took another deep breath and blew again. This time, the sound of a whistle came from her lips. Not just an ordinary whistle, but a repetitive, shrill shriek, the call of a *large* bird.

*Boom!*

Swinging the timber harder and faster than she ever had, Elizabeth rocketed the rawhide deep to left-center garden. As it traveled through the air, the baseball soared like an eagle, like the eagle it was appearing to *follow*.

"Look!" Graham pointed to the heavens, where the great bird seemed to be flying in tandem with the ball.

Farther and farther the baseball (and bird) flew. The ball didn't come back down to terra firma until it reached the shrubs beyond the fans, many yards past where the Pelican player's first shot had landed.

"Mom won!" Griffith exclaimed.

"There is a tomorrow!" Ruby shouted.

"Five down, zero to go!" cheered Graham.

He charged onto the green oasis, and this time, Scribe made no effort to hold him back. Griffith, Ruby, and all the Travelin' Nine stormed the field too. Everyone wanted to congratulate Elizabeth.

At home plate, Graham leaped into his mother's arms, and then Scribe lifted both mother *and* son onto his shoulder. Woody and Bubbles danced in circles, while Doc, the Professor, and Tales tossed their caps into the air. Happy even wheeled Uncle Owen onto the pitch.

"Huzzah!" he managed to murmur. It was the first word anyone had heard him speak all day.

The cranks joined the celebration too. Rushing in from all directions, they surrounded the barnstormers.

"Sweep! Sweep!" the hometown fans cheered. "Sweep! Sweep!"

Elizabeth Payne had accomplished the impossible. There *would* be a baseball match between the New Orleans Pelicans and the Travelin' Nine. On top of that, Elizabeth had helped the barnstormers raise nearly two hundred dollars.

But today wasn't really about the money. Today was about tomorrow.

The Chancellor and his goons didn't stick around for the celebrating. In fact, Griffith spotted them leaving even before Elizabeth's sensational star chaser rolled to a stop.

"What was that?" Griffith pulled his sister aside.

Ruby knew exactly what he was talking about. She shrugged.

"Since when do you know how to whistle?" he asked.

"I don't!" Ruby replied, squeezing the baseball in her pocket. "Well, I didn't know I could! Who knew?"

"I'm not . . ." Griffith stopped.

Over Ruby's shoulder, he spotted Josiah. He was back in the right-field corner again, where Griffith had seen him earlier. A rush of relief surged through him. While the old man may not have been celebrating like everyone else, he was safe, and when his eyes met Griffith's, he nodded.

Spinning back around toward the stadium, Griffith saw that the eagle had returned to his perch high atop Crescent City Base Ball Park as well. But at the moment, the great bird was motioning to the main tent area.

"Wait here," Griffith said to Ruby.

"Where are you going?"

He held up a finger. "I'll be right back. I promise."

With one shoulder lowered and one elbow extended, Griffith barreled through the rush of cranks still swarming to congratulate his mother. He sidestepped strollers, fought through families, and even hopped over held hands as he made his way toward the tent area.

He stopped dead in his tracks just as the entrance to the main tent came into view. Several of the Chancellor's men were exiting. Griffith quickly ducked in back of a woman with a parasol and then slid behind a tree. He watched as they headed off in the other direction, waiting until they were completely out of sight.

Finally he headed in.

The tent was virtually empty. All that remained were a long row of stacked chairs and the tables where the admission tickets

Griffith finally had the dreaded answer.

had been for sale earlier in the day.

But then Griffith spotted someone. A lone figure sat on the ground in the far corner, facing the tent pole. His head was buried in his hands.

Slowly and cautiously, Griffith approached. As he neared, the man stood up. He turned around and lowered his hands.

Griffith began to tremble. *What's the matter? What are you doing here? Why aren't you celebrating with the others?* He didn't need to ask any of those questions.

*Some things you just know.*

On wobbly legs, Griffith stepped closer to his once trusted friend and looked under his cap, catching sight of a face torn by anguish, sadness, and guilt. Standing toe-to-toe with the Rough Rider, Griffith finally had the dreaded answer.

"I am not a man of honor," Crazy Feet said.

# 23

★

## *I Am Not a Man of Honor*

am not a man of honor."

With his cap in hand, Crazy Feet stood before his teammates on the now empty practice field. Behind the Travelin' Nine's left scout and beyond the long evening shadows cast by Crescent City Base Ball Park, the last of the cranks could be seen disappearing down the city streets and across the park. But all eyes were on Crazy Feet.

*I am not a man of honor.*

The seven words Crazy Feet had said to

Griffith in the solitude of the tent had been
the first ones from his mouth on the entire
cross-country adventure. They were the first
words the barnstormers heard from him
too.

*I am not a man of honor.*

"I was approached by the Chancellor's
henchmen way back in Cincinnati," he said
somberly but steadily. "I've been following
their directives and providing them with
information ever since."

"What do you mean by following their
directives?" growled Bubbles.

"What type of information?" Tales
snarled.

Crazy Feet ran a forearm over his stubble.
"I lost the footrace before the match in
the River City on purpose." He looked at
Elizabeth. "Unlike you, I didn't run a smart
race. I pulled up at the end instead of running
through the plate." He turned to Graham,

"I am not a man of honor."

still standing in front of Scribe as he had been all day. "And after that game, you confirmed the existence of the baseball."

"All the way back in Louisville?" Woody asked. "When? How?"

"After your incredible game-ending catch," Crazy Feet replied, "we all piled atop one another out in right garden, and when Graham leaped on, he raised the baseball over his head." Crazy Feet held his hat to his chest. "Then Graham hit that blast in Chicago."

"What blast?" Doc asked. "Graham didn't play in the Windy City. He only took fielding practice."

"After practice!" Graham exclaimed. "You saw!"

"I did." Crazy Feet nodded to Graham before addressing Doc. "After practice, Graham and I stayed to gather the equipment. We were missing a bat, so Graham had to go back for it. When he found an extra ball, he took one final cut. Young Graham over here self-hit the ball out of Lake Park and over the buildings on the far side of Michigan Avenue." He faced Elizabeth. "That's when I knew for certain that Graham was who—"

"You relayed all this to the Chancellor's men?" the Professor interrupted, rubbing his eye patch.

Crazy Feet nodded.

"That's why it always seemed like they were one step ahead of us," said Tales.

Crazy Feet's face tightened. "In Chicago, I told them where we were staying." He looked to Griffith. "Your middle-of-the-night encounter—I was responsible for that. In fact, that evening was the first time I'd ever met the Chancellor. Until then, I'd only inter-acted with his henchmen."

Griffith had always wondered how the Chancellor was able to perfectly time their rendezvous. Had Crazy Feet somehow contributed to his restlessness that evening in Chicago? Did Crazy Feet subtly steer him outside?

"How were you doing this?" Bubbles asked angrily. "How were you able to coordinate these secret meetings when you were with us all the time?"

"He wasn't with us all the time," the Professor answered first. "There were many occasions when we weren't together."

"I reckon he could've met with them most any night after we all went to bed," Woody added. "'Cept for the ones when we were ridin' the rails."

"Most of the meetings did take place at night," said Crazy Feet. "Many times I would—"

"Enough!" Elizabeth shouted. "I don't care about how you did it!"

Ruby covered her ears. The fury in her

mother's tone shook Ruby, just like it had earlier in the week when she'd directed her anger at Uncle Owen. Ruby looked to her uncle, hunched over in his wheelchair. Even though he wasn't the cause of Elizabeth's anger this time, he looked as anguished as ever.

"I don't care about how you did it," Elizabeth repeated. She stepped to within inches of Crazy Feet's face. "I want to know *why*. Why would you do such a thing?"

Crazy Feet's shoulders slumped. He lowered his eyes.

"No!" Elizabeth yelled. "Look at me when you explain yourself!"

Slowly Crazy Feet lifted his head. Streams of tears flowed down his cheeks. He then shuffled away from Elizabeth so that all the barnstormers could see him.

"The Chancellor has my family."

Elizabeth covered her mouth and gasped.

Crazy Feet nodded. "He has my wife and four children. If I don't do everything he says, he'll harm them." Crazy Feet paused as his tears fell faster. "I had no choice."

"Why didn't you tell us?" asked Ruby.

"We would've helped you," the Professor added, motioning to the Paynes. "Just like we're helping Guy's family. How could you not trust your fellow Rough Riders?"

"I couldn't ask for your help." Crazy Feet shook his head. "The henchmen told me that if anyone learned of their kidnapping, the Chancellor would—he would start *eliminating* them one at a time. Beginning with my youngest."

Elizabeth let out an audible squeal from beneath her hand. Then she reached for Griffith and Ruby and pulled them close.

"I put my family before this family," Crazy Feet went on. "It was the most difficult decision I ever had to make, betraying you and—" Crazy Feet's voice broke. He took several long breaths before continuing. "It's the reason I haven't spoken. Not only did I fear accidentally saying something that would've endangered my loved ones, but I also knew that no matter what words left my lips, they wouldn't have been entirely truthful." He swallowed. "So I chose silence. Total silence."

Preacher Wil stepped over to Crazy Feet. He placed a hand on the left scout's shoulder and whispered in his ear.

Griffith and Ruby strained to listen, but they couldn't hear what he said.

"Thank you," Crazy Feet murmured to Preacher Wil. "That means a lot, but I don't think I ever will."

"Yes, you will," Preacher Wil assured him.

"My conscience finally got the best of me in St. Louis," Crazy Feet went on, addressing the Travelin' Nine again. "I was instructed to lose the Sprint Across the River, but I couldn't. I'd had enough of not trying my hardest. I'd failed to give it my all in Louisville, Chicago, and Minneapolis, but no more." Crazy Feet stood up taller. "I won that footrace in defiance of the Chancellor."

"But what about your family?" Doc asked. "What about the Chancellor's threat?"

Crazy Feet's tears flowed faster. "I told myself I'd provided the Chancellor with far more than—I'd gone above and beyond. But the Chancellor—" He took several breaths and peeked at Truman, who had made his way over and sat down by his feet. "I made that decision in the heat of the moment, but it is one that has pierced my soul with fear ever since, because my reasoning—I *still* underestimated the cruelty of the Chancellor."

"I reckon the Chancellor canceled the game in St. Louis because you won the race," said Woody. "And of course he's been tryin' to derail us the entire time we've been here in New Orleans."

"Woody's right," Crazy Feet added. "The Chancellor doesn't see things like—I won't ever again believe a single word that he or any of his henchmen say." He paused for a long moment. "My fellow Rough Riders, I am prepared to do whatever is necessary to save my family. Even if that means sacrificing my own life."

"Is there anything we can do?" Happy asked.

"How can we help?" said Woody.

"I must leave the team," Crazy Feet said. "I must find my wife and children."

"Do you know where they are?" Ruby asked.

"I have some thoughts," replied Crazy Feet, "but I don't know for sure. Since the Chancellor and so many of his henchmen are here in New Orleans, my best chance to save them is now." He swallowed, then whispered so softly Griffith almost didn't hear it. "That is, if they're still alive."

"You must leave the team, Crazy Feet," the Professor said, stepping forward. "But not solely for the reason you stated."

Crazy Feet nodded. "I understand."

"I'm sure you do," Scribe said, "but you still must hear it from one of us. I will take the liberty of speaking for the Rough Riders." He stepped away from Graham and stood next to the Professor. "Crazy Feet, you have violated a trust. You wronged your fellow teammates, your fellow man. This was a betrayal."

"I understand," Crazy Feet repeated.

The Professor reached up and rested his hand on Scribe's shoulder. "Sadly, if you wanted to stay on the team, we couldn't allow it, because we couldn't trust you."

"I understand," Crazy Feet uttered for

a third time. "I don't wish to make this any more difficult or painful. I will say my good-byes and be on my way."

Crazy Feet stepped over to Elizabeth first. He stood before her and stared into her eyes, eyes that contained both anger and understanding.

"I am so sorry," he whispered, and bowed his head.

Elizabeth said nothing. Her blazing eyes said everything.

Next Crazy Feet shuffled over to Graham and waved for Griffith and Ruby. He wrapped his arms around the three Paynes, just like he'd seen Elizabeth huddle her children in close so many times these past weeks. He kissed the tops of their heads.

"Be together," he whispered. "Always."

Crazy Feet then stepped away and faced his teammates. He stood up tall, brought his legs together, raised a hand to his forehead, and saluted his fellow soldiers. He held his pose for a long moment before turning to leave.

As he pivoted away, his head and shoulders held stiffly at an odd angle and his eyes fixed on the green oasis, Uncle Owen began to wheel his chair toward him. However, Owen only managed to move a few feet before slumping forward.

Crazy Feet caught him.

The two veterans hugged, and while locked in their embrace, Crazy Feet whispered in Uncle Owen's ear.

None of the barnstormers were able to hear what was said. But everyone saw Uncle Owen sit up taller than at any point since he'd sat back down in his chair on the pier when the barnstormers had first arrived in New Orleans.

# 24

★

## Pregaming

**othing's   stopping** me from playing today!" Graham declared as he hopped over the railing and onto the green oasis of Crescent City Base Ball Park.

"Playing right garden for the Travelin' Nine," Griffith announced, cupping his hands around his mouth and talking like a circus ringmaster, "Graham Payne!"

"You got that!"

With Crazy Feet gone, the barnstormers

once again had needed a replacement player. After a brief discussion back at Happy's yesterday evening, the team unanimously agreed that that ballist should be Graham. Since the youngest Payne had played right scout at practice, Woody volunteered to shift over to left garden.

Graham brushed some specks of dirt from the sleeve of his jersey and adjusted the cuff. Wearing his birthday present for the first time, he was determined to show his teammates and everyone else that he belonged on the field.

However, the club had been unable to reach a consensus as to where Graham should bat in the lineup. The lively debate had continued on the streetcar ride to the stadium.

"If I'm taking Crazy Feet's place," Graham asserted, swinging around the brass safety pole, "then I need to bat leadoff."

"I contend that Preacher Wil should start things off," the Professor argued. "He may be our hurler, but as we all saw back in Minneapolis, he's solid with the stick."

"I'd like to see Elizabeth in the eighth hole and Graham batting ninth," Doc stated. "Our opposition may think less of a lineup featuring a woman followed by a boy. With those two hitting back-to-back, they won't know what hit them. The two Paynes should bat one right after the other."

STICK: *baseball bat. Also called "lumber" (see page 87) or "timber" (see page 88).*

"I need to bat leadoff," Graham repeated, shaking his head. "I missed out in St. Louis, and don't forget, it's still my birthday week."

"What does that have to do with anything?" Ruby eyed her brother sideways. "Those aren't reasons that—"

"I have a tiny strike zone," Graham interrupted. "I can work out walks and get on base. That's exactly what you want out of your table setter. I have good wheels, too. If

Tales follows me with a base hit, I'm going from first to third no matter where he places the pill. And if I'm hitting leadoff, I don't disrupt the order. Everyone else hits in their usual place in the lineup." He rolled his neck and made a face at Ruby. "Are those more *acceptable* reasons?"

It wasn't until the team reached the plaza in front of the ballpark that Elizabeth proposed the compromise order that all the ballists could agree upon. Graham would bat in the leadoff slot, and Elizabeth would hit last, thus enabling the two Paynes to step to the line one right after the other. Preacher Wil would move up one slot to the eighth position. Even though he was a skilled batsman, he preferred to remain in the bottom third of the order. The rest of the lineup—Tales, Woody, Scribe, Doc, Professor Lance, Bubbles—would remain the same.

**STEP TO THE LINE (v.):** *to prepare to hit.*

"He looks great out there," Griffith said to

Ruby as they stood in front of the Travelin' Nine dugout and watched their younger brother take fielding practice.

Ruby beamed. "Especially wearing that cap and jersey."

Even though it was only warm-ups, Graham chased after every sky ball hit to right garden like it was the most important catch he'd ever needed to make. Then, after making the grab, he'd fire the pill to the infield, throwing it low and hitting the cut-off man each time.

Ruby glanced over at Josiah, Happy, Uncle Owen, and Truman, seated at the far end of the dugout. They, too, were focused on Graham in right garden, and they looked just as proud. Especially Uncle Owen.

Smiling, Ruby gazed around the stadium. On this glorious day, not a single empty seat remained in all of Crescent City Base Ball Park. Babies and children (some small, some not so small) sat on their parents' laps, and the overflowing crowd lined the rows. The young band of musicians who had arrived before anyone else just so they'd be able to sit and play and watch from the front row of the right garden corner prepared to perform their first songs.

That six-boy band broke into a rousing march as the Pelicans took the field. The stadium shook with the crowd's enormous roar.

But Griffith noticed right away that something was off.

"They only have eight players," he said.

Ruby pointed to the hill. "Why is their hurler heading toward first sack?"

"I don't like the looks of . . ."

Griffith couldn't finish his sentence.

Ruby brought one hand to her chest and lowered the other onto the baseball in her pocket. She gasped.

The greatest pitcher in the game had stepped out onto the field and was heading for the mound.

# 25

★

## *Li'l Woody*

y Young!" **Griffith**
exclaimed.

"What are you doing
here?" the Professor
called to the ace hurler as he headed to
the hill.

"I couldn't pass up the opportunity to
throw against the most famous team in all
the land," he replied.

Griffith ran a hand over his mouth. When
he'd learned the others had met and seen the
great pitcher practice back in St. Louis, he

had been disappointed he'd missed out. But he was hardly pleased to see him now.

"But why aren't you with the Superstars?" Woody asked.

Cy Young stopped in front of the bump. "Some men approached me after my game yesterday and asked me to pitch in this here match. They said they'd cover all my expenses if I did, and they even swore up and down to my manager that they'd have me back in time for my game tomorrow in Vicksburg, Mississippi." He backpedaled up to the rubber and began stretching out his pitching arm. "They promised me a boatload in bonus money if I beat you guys," he added, smiling and flexing his eyebrows.

Ruby looked over at the Rough Riders. She expected to see a row of frustrated faces, but instead she didn't see a single expression of disgust or contempt. The barnstormers all understood that this pitching change had everything to do with the Chancellor and nothing to do with Cy Young. The ace hurler wasn't another one of the Chancellor's pocket pawns. He was a professional baseball player, a fierce competitor who never shied from a challenge on the playing field.

"Look on the bright side," said Ruby, turning to Griffith and trying to sound upbeat. "You're getting to see the great Cy Young pitch."

Griffith half nodded and half shook his head. "I would've preferred it under different circumstances," he muttered. Then he added, "Look who's here." He pointed to the stands.

Behind the Pelicans dugout, a dozen dark-suited men were slowly making their way through the cranks toward a roped-off section. Griffith, Ruby, and the others had been so focused on Cy Young that they didn't notice them until they'd nearly reached their seats.

"Is he there?" Ruby asked. "I don't see him."

Griffith knew she meant the Chancellor. "He has to be," he replied, even though Griffith couldn't spot him among the sea of similarly dressed thugs pushing their way to the front.

It wasn't until a pair of men held up the rope so that the Chancellor could pass under that Griffith and Ruby finally saw him.

**ON-DECK AREA:** *place on the field between the dugout and home plate where the next scheduled hitter awaits his turn to bat.*

As the Chancellor and his men found their seats, Griffith glanced over at Josiah, sitting on the Travelin' Nine bench. He had ducked behind Scribe's mammoth frame, trying to remain out of sight. Griffith wondered how the old man planned to stay hidden from view when the barnstormers were out in the field.

"It's almost time!" Graham declared, bounding toward the on-deck area in front of the barnstormers' bench.

"You know what to do up there," said Griffith.

Graham took a couple of practice swings and then turned back toward his brother and sister. "I sure do, but give me a chance."

"Why wouldn't we?" Ruby asked.

Graham rested his lumber on his shoulder. "Don't use the baseball yet," he said. "I want to do this on my own."

"I don't know, Grammy," Griffith said. "We can't risk it. We have to do everything we can to win—"

"No, Griff," Graham interrupted. "Hold off for now. Please. With me in the game, you may not even need to use the baseball."

"Griff's right," said Ruby, shaking her head and glancing to her older brother. "There's too much at stake for us to be taking chances."

But Graham sensed his siblings were beginning to waver. "Give me a few innings," he pressed. "Let me play against the adults. Please. Let me face Cy Young on my own."

Griffith turned to Ruby. "An at bat or two?"

Ruby nodded. "We have gotten pretty good at using the baseball. I think we can." She pointed to Graham. "But as soon as the Travelin' Nine need help, we're using it."

"*If* they need help," Graham said.

He headed back to the on-deck area.

"May I have your attention, please," the umpire announced. He stepped out from behind home plate and stood between the dish and the hurler's hill. "Ladies and gentlemen, children young and old, it is with great pride and pleasure that I present to you the Travelin' Nine, heroes from the war in Cuba, and our very own New Orleans Pelicans!" He lifted his hat, motioned to the ballists on both squads, and then pointed toward Graham. "Striker to the line!"

"STRIKER TO THE LINE!": *what the umpire announced at the start of each contest. It was also called out at each batter's turn. Today, the umpire yells, "Batter up!"*

345

But Graham Payne didn't respond to the call. Instead he continued taking his practice cuts in front of the barnstormers' bench.

"Striker to the line!" the umpire repeated.

Still Graham didn't react.

"Graham, you're up!" Griffith said.

"Everyone's waiting for you!" Ruby waved her brother to the dish. "Are you nervous?"

"Nervous?" Graham scrunched his face into a knot. "Why would I be nervous?"

"Well, the last time you faced Cy Young, he made you look silly," Ruby answered, chuckling. "He corkscrewed you into the ground!"

Graham scrunched his face into an even tighter knot. "I'm waiting for my proper introduction. This is my first at bat ever!"

"A proper introduction?" asked Ruby. "You've got to be kidding."

Graham pointed to his face. "Does it look like I'm kidding?"

"I reckon I'll go tell the umpire," Woody

said, shaking his head and smiling. He trotted past the three Paynes onto the field.

Graham leaned on his lumber. "I think I need a nickname," he said.

Ruby flipped her hair. "Should we really be discussing this now?"

But Griffith understood exactly what his brother was doing. Graham was trying to stay loose. Their mother liked to juggle to help her relax and focus. Graham liked to joke and play.

"I like the nickname 'Gnat,'" Griffith said with a smile.

"Very funny." Graham lifted his lumber and wagged it at Griffith. "I was thinking of something more along the lines of 'Graham the Great.'"

"I like 'Mouth,'" Ruby said, laughing. "That works for me."

Graham growled. "'Super Kid,'" he fired back.

"How 'bout 'Li'l Woody'?" the Travelin'
Nine's new left scout suggested upon returning from his brief conference with the
umpire.

"I like it!" Graham exclaimed. He raised
his timber over his head. "I'm 'Li'l Woody.'"

Once again, the umpire removed his cap
and addressed Graham.

"Now batting for the Travelin' Nine," the
umpire announced with a big grin, "the right
scout, leadoff hitter Graham 'Li'l Woody'
Payne!"

Before the umpire had even finished saying his name, Graham was digging in at the
dish and sizing up Cy Young.

Griffith peered down the bench toward
his mother. Her hands were under her chin,
her eyes glued to the field. He knew how
nervous she was with Graham on the field
and the Chancellor and his goon squad only
yards away.

On the mound, Cy Young raised his arms high above his head, held his pose for a long moment, and then fired his first pitch. The fastball caught the inside part of the plate.

"Strike one!" the umpire bellowed.

Graham nodded once. As anxious and excited as he was to face Cy Young again, Graham had managed to stick to his strategy, taking the first pitch. Even if it had been exactly where he wanted it (which it wasn't), Graham wasn't swinging.

For the second offering, Graham was sitting on a knee-high fastball. Anything else he was taking again.

Cy Young's second pitch was indeed another heater, but this time around, Graham couldn't lay off. Swinging a second too late, he chased the tailing fastball.

"Strike two!"

Just like back in St. Louis, Graham found himself in an 0–2 hole against the ace hurler.

On the hill, Cy Young smirked as he stared at his backstop for the signs. But he didn't need any signs. Everyone knew what pitch was coming.

Graham swung as hard as he could at the rising fastball, but he had no chance against the high heat. Nor did any batter in baseball.

Once again, Cy Young had fanned Graham on three straight pitches. But this time, it counted.

**FAN (v.):** *to strike out.*

"Never again!" Graham growled as he stormed back to the bench. "That's a promise."

# 26

★

*Dueling Aces*

**y Young retired Tales** on a bug bruiser back to the bump and Woody on a stinger to left, setting aside the Travelin' Nine one-two-three in the top of the first frame.

Graham broke for the field the moment Woody's strike reached Joe Stanley's mitt. Charging onto the green oasis, he crossed into fair territory before any of the Pelican players even left the pitch. At first sack, he stomped the bag with both feet and then sprinted out to right garden, waving to the

**BUG BRUISER:**
*ground ball. Also called "ant killer" (see page 85), "worm burner" (see page 309), "grass clipper" (see page 355), or "daisy cutter" (see page 381).*

**FRAME:**
*inning*

band that was entertaining the crowd.

"Let's go, Preacher Wil!" Graham shouted over the music when he reached his position. "Show 'em what you can do!"

Ruby stood on the dugout bench and looked to the mound. As was the case during the match in Minneapolis, Preacher Wil was all business. Between the white lines, the Travelin' Nine's hurler transformed into a no-nonsense competitor. He didn't care if the opposing ballists were the poorest sports in the land or the nicest gentlemen in the world. Like the great Cy Young, Preacher Wil knew how to play baseball only one way: to win.

**BETWEEN THE WHITE LINES:** *on the playing field, in fair territory.*

**CHOKE UP (v.):** *to hold the bat away from the knob.*

**BUNT:** *soft and short hit, often to advance a runner.*

The first batter Preacher Wil had to face was Joe Stanley. The Travelin' Nine's hurler knew the home team's left scout tried to shrink the strike zone by choking up on the timber, crowding the plate, and hunching over the dish. He also liked to first-pitch bunt occasionally.

Preacher Wil started the Pelicans' leadoff man with a fastball over the heart of the
plate for strike one. Not surprisingly, Stanley
had squared to bunt, but he was taking all
the way, hoping to get a good look at one of
Preacher Wil's pitches. Stanley swung at the
second offering, chasing an outside heater
that he fouled into the crowd down the first
base line. Quickly, the striker found himself
behind in the count 0–2.

Ruby grinned as Preacher Wil placed his
leather over his mouth. She knew that behind
his glove, he was smiling just as wide as she
was. Ruby also knew what pitch would be
coming next—the curveball. The barnstormers' southpaw hurler rocked into his motion,
pivoted into his windup, and unleashed a
massive twelve-to-six hook. Stanley's knees
buckled.

HOOK:
curveball.
Also called
"breaking pitch"
(see page 354) or
"breaking ball"
(see page 404).

"Strike three!"

The Pelicans' second striker didn't fare
much better. Like Joe Stanley, the number

two hitter fell behind 0–2, but unlike the leadoff man, this batter was too baffled by the back-to-back breaking pitches to even swing. Preacher Wil then brought the heat. The hapless hitter finally started his swing *after* the ball reached Elizabeth's glove.

"Strike three!"

**BREAKING PITCH:** *curveball. Also called "hook" (see page 353) or "breaking ball" (see page 404).*

**FOUL TICK:** *foul ball that barely touches the hitter's bat.*

With two out and nobody on, Frenchy Genins stepped to the line. Opening his stance and lowering his front shoulder, Genins was looking to drive the ball to right garden. Showing a little more patience at the plate than his predecessors, the home team's center scout worked the count to two balls and one strike. Then he started fouling off pitches.

Fastball. Foul tick.

Fastball. Foul tick.

Fastball. Foul tick.

Back and forth they dueled, until finally, somehow, Genins connected.

*Crack!*

He lifted a towering star chaser to right garden. Graham was going to have his first play. Fighting the glare of the high sky and shielding his eyes from the summer sun, the young scout tracked the path of the pill. Without ever taking his eyes off the ball, Graham circled under it, pounded his leather, and then with two hands, squeezed it for the final out of the frame.

"Three hands dead!"

Graham flipped the ball into the air, tucked his glove under his arm, and jogged to the bench . . . backward, of course!

Scribe led off the top of the second. First-pitch swinging, the power-hitting center scout tried driving the ball to right. But because Cy Young kept his heater down to the right-handed slugger, Scribe grounded a grass clipper to second bag instead. The gloveman fielded the rock cleanly and gunned it over

**THREE HANDS DEAD:** *three outs.*

**GRASS CLIPPER:** *ground ball. Also called "ant killer" (see page 85), "worm burner" (see page 309), "bug bruiser" (see page 351), or "daisy cutter" (see page 381).*

**GLOVEMAN:** *fielder.*

to Abner Powell at first bag for the out.

With one gone, up stepped Doc Linden. Like Scribe, the Travelin' Nine's third bag man looked to drive a first-pitch fastball. But once again, Cy Young had other plans. He froze Doc with his infamous "slow ball." While cranks traveled far and wide just to see Cy Young fire his overpowering fastball, true baseball minds knew that the ace's changeup was by far his most effective pitch. Since the speed of his slow ball was in such sharp contrast to his heater, bewildered batters—like Doc—had little idea what to expect or how to prepare at the plate. Nevertheless, the barnstormers' third sack man did somehow manage to make contact. On an ugly check swing, Doc blooped a Texas Leaguer over the shortstop's head and just in front of Joe Stanley in left. The striker's excuse-me cut had delivered the Travelin' Nine's first hit of the afternoon.

Even though Doc had reached base safely, Professor Lance, the barnstorm-

**CHANGEUP:** *slow pitch thrown with the exact same arm action as a fastball, designed to disrupt the timing of the hitter.*

**CHECK SWING:** *when a batter starts to swing for the ball, but stops shortly before the ball reaches home plate.*

**TEXAS LEAGUER:** *bloop hit that drops between infielder and outfielder.*

ers' next striker, strolled to the line know-ing that Cy Young was in control. So the visiting hitter decided to go with a differ-ent approach. He tried laying down a bunt. As soon as he squared, Doc took off from first. Unfortunately, bunting was not the Professor's forte, and he popped the pill into the air. Standing on the bump, Cy Young barely had to budge for the basket catch put-out. He then underhanded the rock to first, where he doubled off Doc for the final out of the frame.

**BASKET CATCH:** *catch made with the palm of the glove turned upward and the wrist kept close to the body.*

After firing seventeen pitches in the open-ing inning, Preacher Wil realized he would need to be a much more efficient hurler if he wanted to go the distance. So in that second frame, instead of trying to overpower the hit-ters with his fastball and taxing his elbow with his curveball, he mixed speeds and locations.

Incorporating Cy Young's slow ball into his own pitching arsenal, Preacher Wil struck out the first Pelican on three pitches. Without a doubt, the striker was expecting heaters and hooks, not a trio of changeups.

Fred Abbott was next to the line. Clueless as to what to expect from the crafty hurler, the Pelicans' backstop was guessing all the way . . . and guessing wrong! Preacher Wil painted the inside black for strike one and caught the outside corner for strike two.

**PAINT THE INSIDE BLACK (v.):** *to pitch the ball over the inside edge of the plate.*

Abbot's lumber didn't leave his shoulder on either pitch. With two strikes against him, the hitter needed to swing at anything close. So Preacher Wil delivered a pitch that was close, but not *too* close. Abbott flailed at the high and tailing offering.

"Strike three!" Griffith called at the same time as the umpire.

"Preacher Wil's putting on a show!" Ruby added.

Up stepped Abner Powell. Like Joe Stanley, the Pelicans' player-manager choked up on the lumber and crowded the plate.

But Preacher Wil couldn't care less.

Changeup. Strike one.

Changeup. Strike two.

Changeup. Strike three.

Three hands down. Preacher Wil had struck out the side!

"What a duel!" Griffith said to Ruby as they walked to the far end of the dugout.

"They're both pitching the game they didn't get to throw in St. Louis," Ruby added.

When they reached the end of the bench, Griffith and Ruby were surprised to find Uncle Owen no longer sitting in his wheel-chair. He was on the bench like the other Rough Riders. However, unable to hold himself upright, he leaned against Josiah. Happy stood directly in front of the two men—in case Owen needed additional support and in

**THREE HANDS DOWN:** *three outs.*

**STRIKE OUT THE SIDE (v.):** *to record all three outs in an inning by strikeout.*

order to shield Josiah from the Chancellor.

Ruby peeked back across the field to the Chancellor's sitting area. Surrounded by his men, he was still difficult to spot. But every so often she'd catch a glimpse of him, his arms tightly crossed and his steely glare fixed on the field.

"I can't recall ever seeing a pair of dueling aces put on this kind of show," Uncle Owen said to Griffith and Ruby.

Despite his weakened condition, and even though the Travelin' Nine weren't winning, Uncle Owen beamed with joy. His eyes sparkled and his sun-reddened cheeks glowed.

"Who's going to blink first?" Happy asked.

Uncle Owen looked at Ruby's pocket. "I think the Rough Riders could use a little of this magic I've heard so much about."

Ruby glanced to Griffith and then gazed back at her uncle. "Not yet," she replied. "We promised Graham we'd hold off."

"Maybe Graham will create a little magic of his own," Griffith added.

"Seems like the Rough Riders could use a little help at the dish," said Uncle Owen.

"They could," Griffith agreed, nodding. "But let's give it another inning or two. We owe it to Grammy."

However, in the top of the third, the Travelin' Nine strikers still couldn't hit a lick against Cy Young. For the third straight frame, he set them down in order, retiring Bubbles, Preacher Wil, and Elizabeth on only eight pitches.

Thanks to the slick fielding of each of his outer garden scouts, Preacher Wil was able to set the opposition down one-two-three in the bottom of the frame too. Woody made a galloping one-handed grab of a rising rope to left for the first out. Scribe followed that up by flashing some leather with a boot-string catch of a ball hit to short center. Then with two men down, Cy Young stepped to the dish and blooped a ball into right. Charging full speed toward the line, Graham reached down and made a two-handed catch on the dead run. The Travelin' Nine's rookie right scout was racing so fast his momentum nearly carried him into the trombone player and trumpeter already standing in foul territory and preparing to perform once that third out had been recorded. Graham skipped past the musicians, whirled around, and then darted for the dugout (yes, backward).

However, Graham remained at the barnstormers' bench only long enough to grab his bat, because he was leading off the visiting half of the fourth frame.

This time around, the youngster was determined to stick to his strategy against the great Cy Young. Even though he'd struck out on three pitches in the first, Graham was returning to the dish as confident as ever.

Charging full speed toward the line . . .

*Sluggers*

The only thing he was a little nervous about was remaining patient.

"C'mon, Li'l Woody!" Doc Lindy cheered.

"Show 'em how it's done!" urged Bubbles.

"Let's go, Gnat!" Ruby teased.

Graham shot a glare in her direction and then fixed that same stare on Cy Young. He knew the hurler was expecting him to swing for the fences again, so without a doubt, the fireballer would be bringing his upstairs heat. Graham exhaled a long puff. He had to lay off the high hard ones because he'd learned last time that it was impossible to catch up with one of Cy Young's rising fastballs . . . even if you knew it was coming!

Sure enough, Cy Young threw back-to-back high heaters, but Graham didn't bite at either.

Ball one.

Ball two.

Graham let out a second deep breath. Cy Young had to throw a pitch over the

**FIREBALLER:**
*a pitcher who throws hard.*

dish. Graham had studied the hurler all afternoon—just like Griffith always scouted the opposing pitchers at practices and during games. He knew how Cy Young attacked his hitters. Graham would be waiting for that next pitch—a slow ball at the knees.

*Crack!*

Base hit up the middle!

The Travelin' Nine—except for Tales, who was stepping to the line—stood on the bench and cheered. Even Cy Young tipped his cap to the eight-year-old phenom standing on first sack.

Of course, Owen, Happy, and Josiah hadn't been able to join the others on the bench. Owen applauded as loud as he could from his seated position, while Happy jumped up and down in front of a whistling Josiah.

Leading off first bag, Graham tried to distract Cy Young from Tales. The rookie right scout even drew a couple of throws, but the Pelicans' hurler still fanned the Travelin'

Nine's second sack man on three pitches.

With Woody at the dish, Graham wanted to be in scoring position. But Cy Young knew it too, and the Pelicans' ace was keeping tabs on him at first. Before firing a single pitch, Cy Young made five throws to first, and by the time he delivered that initial offering, Woody was tired of waiting. Overswinging on the fastball, he popped up weakly to short for the second out.

Facing Scribe, Cy Young no longer had to concern himself with the base runner. All he needed to do was take care of the striker at the line, and that's exactly what he did. On a one-strike pitch, Scribe lifted a lazy sky ball to left for the final out.

"How much longer do we wait?" Ruby asked Griffith as the teams switched sides.

"Not much," he replied, glancing at her pocket.

In the bottom half of the inning, the

**SCORING POSITION:** *Any time a runner is on second or third bag, he is considered to be in scoring position.*

Pelicans put their first runner on base too, though Preacher Wil was hardly to blame.

After Joe Stanley fanned for the second time to lead off the frame, the next striker hit a routine grass clipper down to Tales that went right through his legs. Frenchy Genins followed with another easy grass clipper, this time to Bubbles. The usually sure-handed shortstop looked to turn two, but he rushed the play, bobbling the ball and booting it away.

Two infield muffs in one inning!

With two on and one out, the Pelicans' next batter headed for the plate. As he took his practice cuts, there was no doubt he was aiming in Graham's direction. A fly ball to right would almost certainly move the runners over, and a base hit that way would undoubtedly mean the first tally of the match.

"Bring it," Graham whispered, staring down the batter.

After taking the first pitch, the Pelican

**MUFF:** error.

**TALLY:** run scored. On some fields, whenever the home team scored, a tally bell would sound. The tally keeper was the official scorer or scorekeeper.

striker lifted a cloud hunter Graham's way. It looked like another easy play for the right scout. However, because the sky ball was hit fairly deep, it would surely advance the runners. . . .

Not so fast!

Graham circled under the pill. He positioned himself a few feet beyond it, and then, as it began its descent, he charged in. With two hands, he caught the rock, skipped into his crow hop, and uncorked a frozen rope. The throw traveled on a line from right garden, past second base, and through the cutoff man standing near shortstop. On one hop, the pea landed in Doc Lindy's leather at third.

Neither runner advanced!

"What a cannon!" Happy cheered.

"That's my brother out there!" Ruby exclaimed. "Way to throw, Li'l Woody!"

Graham's defensive gem provided Preacher Wil with a much-needed boost.

**FROZEN ROPE:** *hard line drive or throw.*

He worked out of the jam by retiring Fred Abbott on another three-pitch strikeout.

"I think the Travelin' Nine could use a little magic," Ruby said to Griffith as the barnstormers headed back to the bench.

Griffith tapped his temple. "Great minds think alike."

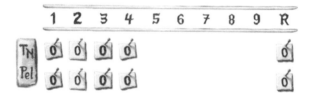

# 27

★

## Music and Magic

s **Doc stepped out** of the dugout and prepared to lead off the fifth frame, Griffith and Ruby headed back down to the far end of the bench.

"Now it's time for that magic," Ruby said to Uncle Owen, who had returned to his wheelchair because he needed the backrest for support.

"We want all of your help," added Griffith, looking to Happy and Josiah. The old man was still trying to remain hidden from view.

"Tell us what to do," Happy said.

"Griff and I are going to join hands with Uncle Owen on the baseball," she explained, showing the sphere to the Travelin' Nine's former hurler. "We need for you and Josiah to be on watch. We're not sure what the magic's going to look like this afternoon."

"Graham isn't batting for a while," Uncle Owen said, pointing to the youngest Payne standing in front of the dugout. "Have him join us."

Griffith nodded. "I'll be right back," he said.

He hurried over to Graham, who was huddled with Doc, Bubbles, Preacher Wil, and his mother. He was about to pull him away when Griffith realized what Graham was doing. He was *teaching*. Since Graham had been the only one to get a solid hit against the great Cy Young, he was providing pointers.

Yet again, Griffith was surprised by his little brother's maturity.

As he waited for Graham to finish, Griffith gazed out at the group of musicians in the right garden corner. The band of six boys—all of whom appeared to be about the same age as he and Ruby, except for the tiny tuba player, who looked like he was younger than Graham—entertained the crowd as they had all afternoon when the squads switched sides. Many of the nearby cranks danced and sang along.

Then Griffith looked across the diamond. From where he stood, he had a clear line of sight to the Chancellor, surrounded by his dark-suited entourage. The Chancellor sat up tall, his body stiff. He didn't move, he didn't blink. Even from the far side of the field, the Chancellor's agitation and impatience were palpable.

Finally Graham finished holding court,

and as Doc headed for the line, Griffith led his brother over to the others.

Like they had so many times before on their cross-country adventure, Griffith, Ruby, and Graham joined hands on the baseball. Then Ruby waved for Uncle Owen to place his atop theirs.

"On second thought," he said, shaking his head, "let's stick with what's been working."

Was it the three hands on the ball or Ruby's wave that brought the breeze? It blew in from behind the cranks seated in back of home plate and along the infield lines. Rushing over the stands and across the diamond, the steady wind was accompanied by a shrieking whistle that beat against the stadium's rafters and wooden frame like a mallet striking the bars of a xylophone.

*Crack!*

Before any of the three young Paynes could respond to Uncle Owen's decision or the breeze, Doc smacked Cy Young's pitch with the sweet spot of his timber. The soaring star chaser split the alley in left-center garden.

"Run, Doc!" Ruby cheered over the whistling wind.

"Go for three!" Griffith urged.

Doc tore around the bases, and by the time Frenchy Genins chased down the rock and fired it back to the infield, Doc stood on third bag with a stand-up triple.

**ALLEY:** *either of two areas in the outfield, one between left garden and center garden and the other between right garden and center garden.*

"Our second base runner of the afternoon!" Graham declared.

"Bring him home!" called Ruby to the Professor, who was heading for the dish. She brushed her hair from her eyes now that the breeze had subsided. "Put a Travelin' Nine tally on the board!"

"Did you hear the whistling?" Griffith asked, pointing skyward.

"Of course," Graham replied. "It sounded like Ruby's whistle from yesterday."

"It sure did," said Griffith. "I think we should all try whistling with the Professor at the dish."

Ruby shrugged. "It's worth a shot," she said.

As the barnstormers' first sack man set himself at the line, the siblings began to whistle. Never before had any of them generated such melodic sounds. Wide-eyed and hopeful, they focused on Professor Lance, whose glances toward the dugout told the three Paynes he could hear their cheerful chirps.

Unlike Doc, the Professor hadn't heard Graham's batting tips, but with nobody out and the go-ahead run ninety feet away, he knew he needed to be patient at the plate. The Professor worked the count in his favor and waited for a pitch he could drive to the outer garden. However, with three balls and one strike, he popped the pill straight up.

Griffith, Ruby, and Graham whistled harder than ever. The flutelike sounds grew louder.

Suddenly the pop-up began to drift, first over the hill and then beyond the infield dirt. As if carried by the tune, the rock soared toward left garden. While the cloud hunter didn't travel over Joe Stanley's head, it went more than far enough for Doc to tag up. When the pill landed in the fielder's mitt, Doc took off for home and scored easily on the sacrifice fly.

**TAG UP (v.):** to advance to the next base after a fly-ball out.

**SACRIFICE FLY:** fly-ball out that advances a runner.

"The magic is back!" Graham cheered.

"That had nothing to do with magic," Griffith corrected him. "That was baseball by the book."

Ruby eyed Griffith sideways. Even though the barnstormers had employed and executed perfect strategy, without a doubt the whistling had played a part. Why would Griffith deny that? Was he trying not to get his hopes up? Ruby could see her big brother's brain racing.

"Have it your way, Griff," Graham said, thumping his chest. "Doc did exactly what I told him to, and then the Professor—"

"That's the only run they're getting this frame," Griffith cut him off, even though Bubbles had quickly worked out a four-pitch base on balls.

Ruby and Graham looked to their older brother.

"Why on earth would you say such a thing?" asked Ruby.

"Whatever happened to only positive thoughts?" Graham knocked on his older brother's head.

As Graham's words left his lips, Cy Young fired his first pitch to Preacher Wil, who popped a lazy sky ball to Joe Stanley for the second out of the inning.

"I *am* thinking only positive thoughts,"

**BASE ON BALLS:** *walk. If a batter receives four pitches out of the strike zone in one plate appearance, he advances to first base.*

Griffith said. "But they're realistic positive thoughts."

"They sounded pretty negative to me," said Graham.

With Elizabeth heading to the line, Griffith pointed to the hill. "Against a pitcher like Cy Young, you can't get greedy. You have to play the match one tally at a time." He looked down at the hands on the baseball and then at his brother and sister. "It's going to take more than whistling for the barnstormers to beat this hurler. We need to come up with ways to use the baseball."

"Do you think it might have to do with music?" Ruby asked, peeking at the band down the right garden line.

Griffith smiled. "That's what I'm beginning to believe."

But before they could do anything, Cy Young retired their mother. Instead of trying to overpower the steady striker, the Pelicans' ace let her put the ball in play. The Travelin' Nine's backstop poked a harmless looping liner to Abner Powell at first.

Three hands dead.

The musicians down in right garden struck their first chords even before the Pelicans' first sack man squeezed his glove. The band members had only a short time to play between each frame, and they wanted to make the most of every second.

As Graham and the other ballists headed out onto the green oasis, Ruby and Griffith sat down on the bench, near where Josiah was attempting to stay out of view.

"I'm convinced there's a connection between music and the baseball," Griffith said, scratching his chin.

Ruby nodded.

"Music is more than just sounds and instruments," he continued. "It's about rhythm and tempo, too."

Ruby realized Griffith was thinking out loud as much as he was speaking to her, so she decided to let him talk.

"During other matches, we've pointed the baseball in different directions and shifted it around," Griffith went on. He gazed up at the eagle perched high atop Crescent City Base Ball Park, in the same spot from which he had watched over the skills competition yesterday. "I think that's what we should try to do now." He turned back to Ruby. "If we move the ball around at different speeds while whistling, maybe we can affect or control the action."

Ruby nodded again, eyes on the field.

Already Preacher Wil had gotten into a tight spot. The Pelicans managed to get runners on the corners with only one out and Cy Young stepping in. A sky ball to the outfield could plate a tally and tie up the contest.

"The Travelin' Nine could sure use a ground ball," said Griffith.

**RUNNERS ON THE CORNERS:** *When base runners occupy both first base and third base, a team is said to have runners on the corners.*

"A double-play ball," Ruby added.

"Let me give this a shot."

Griffith took the ball from his sister and watched Preacher Wil size up the tall striker. As soon as the hurler fired the rock, Griffith pointed the baseball toward Doc at third sack and began whistling while shaking it downward. Cy Young swung.

*Crack!*

The batter smoked a daisy cutter toward the hole between shortstop and third. A surefire base hit! But Griffith, who was still shaking the baseball, started pulling it back and shaking it slower. He lowered the tempo of the tune he was whistling too. Suddenly the batted ball slowed down, and after one hop, it appeared to pause in midair. It stopped just long enough so that Doc was able to snare the pill on the run. He fired the rock to second, where Tales caught the throw and then flung the rawhide over to Professor Lance at first.

**DAISY CUTTER:** *ground ball. Also called "ant killer" (see page 85), "worm burner," (see page 309), "bug bruiser (see page 351)," or "grass clipper" (see page 355).*

**HOLE:** *space between two infielders.*

"Inning over!" Ruby cheered. "You did it!"

"We did it," said Griffith over the sounds of the six-boy band, which began to jam the moment the ball reached the Professor's leather.

"That's what I call music!" Ruby exclaimed as the Travelin' Nine trotted from the field. "An around-the-horn double play!"

**AROUND THE HORN:** *throwing the baseball around the infield.* In the dugout, Griffith and Ruby explained to Graham what they'd figured out so far. But since he was leading off the top of the sixth frame, they didn't have a lot of time. Nevertheless, Graham was able to understand that by manipulating the baseball, his brother and sister had impacted the action on the field.

"The magic *is* back!" Graham declared, as he had during the previous frame.

"It sure is," Ruby agreed.

"Time for a big inning," Griffith announced.

"Are you sure, Griff?" asked Graham, smiling his mischievous smile. "You can't get greedy against a hurler like Cy Young," he mocked. "You have to play the match one tally at a time."

"Go hit," Griffith growled, pushing his brother toward the plate. "You're up! We need to figure out how to use the ball."

"Pretend the baseball is an instrument," said Graham, pointing his lumber to the musicians. "When I'm at the line, make like you're playing the drums on the ball."

Ruby's eyes widened. "That's it!" she exclaimed as her younger brother stepped to the line. "Let's *play* the baseball."

"I like the way that sounds," Griffith added, leading his sister to the end of the bench.

"When Graham's about to swing," Ruby said, "we'll beat the baseball." They positioned their hands. "Maybe this will give him more power at the plate."

*Sluggers*

"Mr. Griffith and Miss Ruby," said Josiah, stepping to them but still ducking behind the other ballists, "permit me to hold the sphere. I overheard your plan. When playing percussion, four hands will generate more power."

Ruby placed the ball in the old man's cupped hands.

On the field, Graham settled in at the plate, and when he looked up at Cy Young, Griffith and Ruby pretended to play. Instantly the banging of drums reverberated off the rafters. Griffith and Ruby startled even themselves, and the Travelin' Nine on the bench jumped as one.

"As soon as he's about to make contact," Griffith said excitedly, "strike the baseball as hard as you can."

The hurler rocked into his delivery, and right before Graham swung, Griffith and Ruby drummed the baseball as hard as Josiah could handle.

*Boom!*

Graham blasted Cy Young's first offering of the frame to the deepest part of center garden. Frenchy Genins turned to give chase, but the scout stopped after just a single step. The titanic four-bagger was long gone, traveling nearly as far as Elizabeth's last blast during the Heavy Lumber Longest Strike contest.

"Home run!" Ruby declared.

"Two tallies for the Travelin' Nine, none for New Orleans!" Griffith shouted, lifting the baseball from Josiah's hands and holding it high.

FOUR-BAGGER: home run. Also called "round-tripper" (see page 392).

As Graham raced around the sacks, the cranks cheered wildly. Of course the fans were rooting for the home team, but they had to stand up and applaud what the littlest member of the Travelin' Nine had accomplished against Cy Young. And from the look on the hurler's face, no one had ever hit one of his pitches that far.

"Keep it going!" Graham urged Tales as

he stomped on home plate with both feet.

The barnstormers rushed to congratulate Graham upon his return to the dugout, but by the time they had finished showering him with praise, Tales had already lifted a routine sky ball to Joe Stanley in left for the first out.

"You were right," Ruby said to Graham. The three kids were huddled around their ball again. "Using the baseball as a musical instrument did the trick."

"So let's try it again," said Graham. He glanced at Woody, who was taking his practice cuts as he strode to the plate, and then back at his siblings. "What instrument should we play?"

Griffith gazed at the musicians in the outfield stands. "The bass," he said, passing the ball to his younger brother.

"Yes!" Graham said.

For Woody's entire at bat, Graham pretended to play the bass. On the fourth pitch,

Woody swatted an ant killer down to Abner Powell. It looked to be an easy play, but suddenly the deep-sounding riffs shook the sod and redirected the rock over his glove and down the line. By the time the right scout retrieved the rock, Woody had motored all the way around to third.

"My turn!" Ruby announced, clapping for the baseball.

Graham flipped it to her. "See what you can do," he said, beaming.

But Griffith, for the moment, had stopped enjoying what was taking place between the white lines. "Someone's not happy," he said, pointing across the diamond.

An inning earlier, he had watched as the Chancellor bristled and stiffened, impatient with what was transpiring on the pitch. Now that impatience had turned to fury. Even though the Chancellor's thugs huddled closer than ever, his mouth was visible under the brim of his hat, which covered most of his face. He showed his teeth like an angry grizzly.

Griffith faced the barnstormers' bench again. Josiah stood at the corner of the dugout behind a large wooden support post.

"The Chancellor's losing this game," Graham said defiantly, "and we're winning a lot of money."

"Don't get ahead of yourself, little brother," cautioned Griffith. "This is only the sixth frame, and there's lot of—"

". . . baseball left to be played," Graham finished Griffith's sentence. "You always tell me that, but this afternoon's different, Griff."

"It ain't over till it's over." Griffith, Ruby, and Graham all turned to see Uncle Owen, who had wheeled up next to them. He had a big smile on his face. He was getting to see his fellow soldiers play great baseball, he was getting to see his brother's children create their magic, and he was savoring every moment of this afternoon.

"It ain't over till it's over," Griffith repeated the refrain, and gently placed his hand on his uncle's shoulder.

But even as Griffith said the words, he agreed with Graham. There was something different about today's match. Everything felt right. He glanced over at Ruby. She felt it too.

*Some things you just know.*

"Keep this rally going," said Uncle Owen. "Make this old man happy."

Like Griffith had before, Ruby looked to the band for inspiration. "I've always wanted to try playing the trombone," she said.

"Make some music!" Graham urged.

All three looked to Scribe at the dish. With one out and Woody on third, and the Travelin' Nine now leading by the score of

2–0, he prepared to face Cy Young.

Ruby raised the baseball and waited for Scribe to swing.

*Crack!*

The huge center scout laced a liner straight at Joe Stanley in left garden. The hometown gloveman wouldn't have to take a step to make the catch. . . .

But then Ruby began *playing* the baseball as if it were a trombone. As she pretended to move the imaginary slide back and forth, the batted ball began to dance and flutter, mimicking Ruby's motions and her music. When she extended her imaginary slide, the ball soared high; when she brought it back close, the ball dipped low. To Stanley, the frozen rope seemed to have a mind of its own. Confused and concerned, he covered his face with his mitt, and instead of snaring the pill, he let it pass over his head.

"Run!" the Rough Riders cheered.

Woody easily crossed the dish with the Travelin' Nine's third tally, while Scribe tore around the bags. Joe Stanley turned tail and gave chase, but he had no idea which way the bounding ball was about to bounce. Since Ruby was still tromboning, one moment it hopped left and the next second it skipped right. At one point, the ball jumped backward. By the time the left scout *tackled* the pinballing pill, Scribe had circled the bases for an inside-the-park home run.

"Four nothing!" Graham exclaimed.

"That's what I call a rally," Uncle Owen added, grinning.

Cy Young settled down and retired Doc Linden and Professor Lance on back-to-back strikeouts, closing out the frame. But the three runs he yielded to the Travelin' Nine that inning were the most he'd given up in one frame all year.

Preacher Wil's stellar pitching continued

in the home half of the inning. He fanned Joe Stanley, and then got the second hitter to lift a lazy skyscraper to Woody in left for the next out. However, even the best hurlers on their best days aren't pitch-perfect and will make a mistake a two. Against Frenchy Genins, Preacher Wil left a curveball out over the plate, and the batter blasted the hanging hook over the wall in left for a solo round-tripper and the Pelican's first tally of the afternoon.

After the four-bagger, Griffith wondered if Preacher Wil would try a little chin music on the next striker. However, he realized the Travelin' Nine's hurler knew better. With everything going so well, why give the opposing team a reason to get riled? But by the same token, Griffith decided it couldn't hurt to lend the southpaw a hand.

"Let's see if we can add a little movement to his pitches," he said to Ruby.

**SKYSCRAPER:** *fly ball to the outfield, or outer garden. Also sometimes referred to as "sky ball" (see page 87), "cloud hunter" (see page 89), or "star chaser" (see page 95).*

**ROUND-TRIPPER:** *home run. Also called "four-bagger" (see page 385).*

**CHIN MUSIC:** *pitched ball intentionally thrown high and inside, near the batter's chin and neck.*

She passed him the baseball. "What instrument should we try now?"

Griffith peeked down the right garden line toward the band and started to smile. "Let's play the drums again," he suggested. "This time I'll hold the ball. Pretend your index fingers are drumsticks."

"Sounds good to me," said Ruby.

For Preacher Wil's first offering, Ruby played a rapid-fire staccato rhythm. As the pitch sailed toward the plate, it fluttered about, and even though the rock dissected the dish, the striker's timber never left his shoulder. The batter was far too amazed by the shimmying pill.

"Strike one!" the umpire called.

Ruby beamed. "Now watch this," she said to Griffith.

As Preacher Wil swayed into his motion, Ruby began drumming with her pointers again. This time, however, she played very slowly, raising her fingers nearly to her eyebrows before lowering them to the ball. Preacher Wil released the rawhide, and as it soared toward home plate, the offering seemed to *bounce* in midair, swooping high and dipping down. For the second straight pitch, all the striker could do was watch the rock pass him by.

"Strike two!"

"You're making his magnificent pitches impossible to hit," Griffith said to his sister. "Keep it up."

Ruby nodded once and studied Preacher Wil. While the southpaw rocked into his motion, she began to play the staccato beat again, just like she had on the first pitch. As the ball left his hand, it immediately began to shimmy. But this time around, the batter was ready for the unusual movement. Cocking his bat, he prepared to take his cut, and as soon as he did, Ruby stopped drumming.

Suddenly the pitched ball seemed to *hiccup* in midflight. The batter swung, but Ruby had tinkered with his timing.

"Strike three!" the umpire bellowed. "Three hands dead!"

Preacher Wil had gotten out of the sixth yielding with just the lone tally. With the match moving to the seventh, the Travelin' Nine led by three.

In that seventh frame, Cy Young retired the Travelin' Nine so quickly that the kids— who were engrossed in a strategy session— didn't even have the chance to use their baseball. Then, in the bottom of the inning, Preacher Wil finally began showing some signs of fatigue. After setting aside the first striker on a sky ball to Scribe, he issued back-to-back walks, his first two base on balls of the afternoon.

"He's lost a little control of his breaking pitches," Griffith said.

"I think I might be able to take care of that," said Ruby, rubbing the baseball.

"You sure did last inning."

"Time to play the trombone again."

With each one of Preacher Wil's offerings to the next hitter, she pretended to play the horn, moving the make-believe instrument's slide in the direction of the thrown ball. All of a sudden, Preacher Wil's pitches were curving and breaking the way they had during the early innings, and the southpaw hurler struck out the Pelican batter.

But with two outs and runners still on first and second, the next hitter, Cy Young, connected and lashed a single to left. Ruby thought fast. Still pretending the ball was a trombone, she started playing a slow, frumpy march. When she did, the runners slowed to the point that it seemed like they were trudging through mud. Even though both runners had been off on contact, since there were two outs, Woody easily forced

the lead ballist at third for the final out of
the frame.

Dancing to the music that *everyone* could
hear, the Travelin' Nine returned to the dugout for the start of the eighth inning. The
barnstormers already by the bench bopped
to the beats too.

"What are you doing?" Ruby asked, eye-
ing Griffith sideways.

"What does it look like I'm doing?" Griffith
replied. "I'm dancing, like everyone else."

"You call that dancing?" Ruby covered
her laugh. "It looks like—"

"Don't say another word," he warned,
playfully shaking his fist.

"Say another word about what?" asked
Graham, joining his brother and sister in the
dugout.

Ruby flipped the baseball into the air, but
Graham snared it before she did.

"Don't use it this half inning," Graham

Griffith . . . began whistling while shaking it downward.

said, waving it at his siblings. "I want to face Cy Young on my own." He tossed the ball to his older brother.

Griffith draped an arm over Graham's shoulder and looked to Ruby. She nodded once, and Griffith understood. She was as proud of Graham as he was, and for the top of this frame, they would once again refrain from using their baseball. It wasn't the smartest strategy, with only a three-run lead and so much on the line. It was even a little dangerous. But Griffith and Ruby felt they owed it to their brother. If the Travelin' Nine didn't come through on their own, they would go right back to using the baseball in the bottom of the frame.

The Travelin' Nine didn't come through on their own.

Pop-up.

Strikeout.

Cloud hunter.

Once again, Cy Young set aside the Rough Riders in order.

"Help protect our lead," Graham said. He tipped his cap to his brother and sister as he headed to right garden for the bottom of the frame.

"Will do, Li'l Woody," said Griffith, handing the baseball off to Ruby.

"It's tuba time!" Ruby exclaimed. She pointed to the smallest band member with the largest instrument.

"Big backup from the biggest horn!" Griffith declared. Then he added, "All we need are six more outs."

Raising the baseball to her mouth, Ruby prepared to pretend.

The Pelicans sent the top third of their order to the plate against Preacher Wil. Their first batter, Joe Stanley, ripped a daisy cutter toward the hole between third and shortstop. Doc dove for the rock, but it eluded his leather.

Ruby took a deep breath and then made like she was buzzing the mouthpiece. Suddenly deep bass sounds shook the sod. The bounding bug bruiser boinged toward Bubbles, who backhanded the baseball. Leaping into the air like a ballerina, the sure-handed shortstop fired the pill across the diamond—a perfect strike to Professor Lance for the first out of the frame.

"Bubbles! Bubbles!" shouted Griffith.

While Preacher Wil toed the rubber and readied to face the number two ballist in the lineup, Ruby decided to go with a different approach. This time, she would flap her lips just as the striker started his swing.

"Wait until the second or third offering," Griffith instructed his sister. "This hitter likes to take a pitch or two."

Ruby buzzed the mouthpiece when the

Suddenly deep bass sounds shook the sod.

batter took his cut at the one-one breaking ball. The low note rang out and reverberated off the rafters. The striker swung so slowly it looked like he was whipping the willow through water, and he popped the ball straight into the air. Elizabeth made a basket catch for out number two.

As Frenchy Genins headed to the plate, Griffith turned to Ruby. "Do that again," he suggested.

Ruby nodded. "That was fun."

An aggressive Genins went after Preacher Wil's first pitch, and as she had with the previous batter, Ruby buzzed the mouthpiece. As the low note echoed through the stadium, Genins swung the timber even slower than the last hitter. He may have been aiming for the fences, but the ball left his lumber like a bunt. With catlike reflexes, Elizabeth leaped out from behind the plate, flipped off her mask, barehanded the ball, and slung it to first.

Three hands dead.

**BREAKING BALL:** *curveball. Also called "hook" (see page 353) or "breaking pitch" (see page 354).*

**WHIP THE WILLOW (v.):** *to swing the bat.*

"One inning to go!" Ruby declared.

"We need insurance runs!" Griffith clapped as hard as he could as the barnstormers returned to the bench.

"Time for another big inning!" added Ruby, pulling the baseball from her pocket and waving Graham over.

As Scribe stepped to the line for the start of the final frame, the three siblings joined hands on their baseball.

"Why don't you try making some music?" Ruby said to Graham, with Scribe taking ball one.

The youngest Payne thought for a moment. "I think I'll try the trumpet." He held the baseball high as Scribe watched strike one cross the plate.

"Better yet," said Griffith, "why don't you play the bugle? Since the Rough Riders are military men, I'm sure they're used to hearing its call."

Right away, Graham made like he was

blowing into a bugle, and Scribe responded to the familiar horn call. He swung mightily, and the rock *charged* from his timber. He lashed a sharp worm burner down the third base line. The blistering grounder caromed off the fence in front of the fans and eluded Joe Stanley, allowing Scribe to cruise into second sack with a leadoff double.

"Well done! Let's see what else you can do," Ruby said to Graham.

"I've always wanted to try the flute," he said as Doc prepared for his plate appearance.

But instead of playing when Doc swung the lumber, Graham decided he would wait until the Travelin' Nine's third sack man made contact and began to run.

Good thing, because Doc didn't swing!

Hoping to move Scribe ninety feet closer to home, Doc squared to bunt. However, he pushed the pill a little too hard and right at the third sack man.

Graham started fluting away, an up-tempo, high-pitched whistle.

The fielder gloved the rock cleanly, but when he looked up, he saw Doc racing to first faster than any ballist could possibly run.

Realizing his playing was giving Doc Crazy Feet–like speed, Graham blew harder and faster.

The Pelicans' fielder double-clutched. His short-armed and errant throw ricocheted off Abner Powell's mitt. Scribe, who was running as soon as ball met bat (and almost as fast as Doc, thanks to the flute), never broke stride and crossed the dish with the Travelin' Nine's fifth run of the afternoon.

GINGER: hustle and enthusiasm.

"Now that's what I call ginger!" Griffith declared, pumping his fists at Doc, who had hustled down to second on the muff.

"Keep it going, Professor!" Ruby shouted as the barnstormers' number six hitter made his way to the line.

"With your permission," Graham said to his siblings, "I want to try one more instrument."

"Go for it, Grams!" Griffith exclaimed.

Graham smiled mischievously. If Griffith knew what he had in mind, Graham realized he would never go for it. So before revealing his plan, Graham opted to talk strategy.

"Cy Young's going to throw up and in to Professor Lance," he said.

"What makes you say that?" asked Ruby.

"It's his best weapon against the bunt," he replied matter-of-factly.

"How do you know he's going to bunt?" Griffith wondered.

"A bunt would put Doc on third bag with no outs," Graham explained, pointing with his bat to the green oasis. "All Bubbles would have to do is lift a sky ball to the outer garden, and the Travelin' Nine would have another tally. But if the Professor doesn't bunt, he should move off the plate and take a hack at the high heat."

At the dish, Professor Lance peeked in the direction of the dugout and touched the brim of his cap. He'd heard everything Griffith, Ruby, and Graham had just discussed.

Turning sideways, Graham slid behind his brother.

"What are you doing?" Griffith asked.

"I'm going for it," Graham answered. "When the Professor takes his cut, I'm playing the cymbals. I need to smack the ball against something, but I know you won't let me use your head. So I need your back."

"No way am I letting you use—"

"You just told me to go for it," Graham cut him off.

"I know I did, but—"

"There's no time to argue, Griff!" Ruby interrupted. "The Professor's about to hit."

Moving his back foot off the line, the Professor shifted his weight and raised his front foot so that only the tip of his boot remained on the dirt. He then stared at the ball in Cy Young's hand and waited for the offering. When the ace hurler fired the pitch, it was the rising and tailing fastball that he expected.

Graham was ready too. He banged the baseball against his brother's back. The cymbals' sustained shimmering sound filled Crescent City Base Ball Park.

**WHIP OF THE WILLOW:** *swing of the bat.*

*Crack!*

Driving the ball to the opposite field, Professor Lance's blast soared high and far and way beyond the cranks in right garden.

"Go crazy, folks!" Ruby cheered wildly. "Go crazy! It's a home run!"

"Unbelievable!" Graham shouted. "I don't believe what I just saw!"

With one whip of the willow, the Professor had added two more insurance runs.

Graham raised the baseball high and then stuffed it into Ruby's pocket. All three

Paynes realized they wouldn't be needing it anymore this afternoon.

After the round-tripper, Cy Young settled down and easily retired Bubbles, Preacher Wil, and Elizabeth. But the damage had been done, and the Pelicans would take their last turn at bat against Preacher Wil trailing by six runs.

However, the Chancellor and his men wouldn't be around to see it. With the boy band playing their last between-inning set of the afternoon, they quietly left their seats, made their way back through the crowd, and exited the stands.

**CHANGEOVER:** *the period of time between innings when the teams switch sides.*

Except for the cranks who needed to step out of the way to let them pass, none paid them any mind.

As the thousands and thousands crammed into Crescent City Base Ball Park sang and danced and cheered during the changeover, Ruby peered down the dugout in the direction of Josiah. For the first time all afternoon, he stood in front of the barnstormers' bench, no longer concerned about whether his son would see him. Even from far away, Ruby could see the glimmer of hope in Josiah's eyes. Between the white lines these last two days, the unthinkable had transpired. The Chancellor had met his match and backed off. Did that mean he could be defeated?

**CLEANUP STRIKER:** *player who hits fourth in the batting order.*

Even though the Pelicans came to bat in the bottom of the ninth trailing by six runs and knowing in their hearts they really didn't stand a chance against Preacher Wil, the local ballists weren't about to roll over and concede those last three outs. They made that very clear when their cleanup striker smoked Preacher Wil's first pitch into center garden for a base hit.

"Glad we got those insurance runs," said Griffith.

"Don't worry, Griff," Ruby said. "Preacher Wil has one more masterful half frame left.

He's still going to strike out the side. I'm sure of it."

"I'd love to see that!"

"But if he allows another base runner or two, we're making music with the baseball again."

If Preacher Wil was going to fan the next three batters he faced, he would have to do it with a runner on and the meat of the Pelicans' order coming to the plate.

The southpaw hurler stepped back onto the hill, and like always, he fired his intimidating glare at the next batter, Fred Abbott. Then he brought the heat.

Fastball. Strike one.

Fastball. Strike two.

Fastball. Strike three.

Instead of mixing speeds and changing locations as he had all afternoon, Preacher Wil had stunned Abbott with three straight heaters.

The next Pelican striker, Abner Powell,

had no idea what to expect. Would Preacher Wil continue throwing fastballs? Or would he go back to mixing speeds?

Preacher Wil *toyed* with Abner Powell, throwing a fastball, a changeup, *and* a hook. He had the striker so confused, Powell swung at one offering before it left the ace's hand and another after it popped into Elizabeth's mitt. On the third pitch . . .

**TWO HANDS DOWN:**
*two outs*

"Strike three!" the umpire called. "Two hands down."

**COMPLETE GAME:**
*when the starting pitcher throws every pitch of every inning.*

Preacher Wil was one out away from a complete game. All he had to do was retire one last Pelican striker. He stepped off the mound, ran his fingers over the charm around his neck, and gazed around the stadium. This was *his* moment.

He returned to the hill and toed the rubber. Then Preacher Wil went right after the Pelicans' slugger, challenging him with heaters. The batter managed to foul off a couple of balls, and he even showed some late-game restraint by taking a pitch. But he was clearly overmatched.

"Here comes the curveball," Ruby said to her brothers.

Preacher Wil peeked over at the three Paynes and nodded.

Saving his best for last, Preacher Wil unloaded the most spectacular curveball he'd ever thrown. The batter's knees buckled. His timber never moved.

"Strike three!" the umpire bellowed. "Yer out! The Travelin' Nine win!"

# 28

★

*Huzzah! Huzzah!*

**ver the thunder-**ous roars of the appreciative cranks, Cy Young stood on the pitcher's hill and congratulated the Travelin' Nine.

"This afternoon," he proclaimed, "even I'm willing to concede the better team won."

"Huzzah!" the hometown ballists cheered.

Abner Powell tipped his cap and bowed in Elizabeth's direction. "Madam Payne," he said, "you can play for my squad any time you like."

"Huzzah!" the Pelicans cheered again.

Griffith, Ruby, and Graham hurried over to Happy in the dugout. He was smiling from ear to ear as he gazed at the contents of the crate Cy Young had presented to him prior to addressing the crowd.

"We made a thousand dollars!" Graham exclaimed.

"Probably more," said Griffith, lifting the heavy crate off the bench beside Happy and then placing it right back down. "The stadium holds five thousand fans, and it was standing room only."

"Since all adults paid twenty-five cents to get in," Ruby added, "we definitely earned more money than at all the other games and events on this trip put together!"

Graham's eyes popped out of his head.

"I've never seen so many coins!"

"If we do this well in Charleston and Atlanta," Griffith said, "we just might earn that ten thousand dollars after all."

Uncle Owen, who was seated in his wheelchair in front of Happy, motioned to Ruby. When she stepped forward, he wiggled his fingers in the direction of her pocket. Ruby reached in, removed the baseball, and placed it in her uncle's hand. He stared at the ball for a long moment and then looked up at the Rough Riders, who had now joined them in the dugout.

"May I have everyone's attention?" he asked, his voice a raspy whisper.

He waited for all of the war heroes to face him.

"I would like to dedicate this victory," he said as loudly as he could, "to my brother, who is no longer with us." He brought the baseball to his chest and rested his other hand on his stump. "To the great Guy Payne. Who loved his family, his fellow soldiers, and the game of baseball. Dear brother, I salute you."

"Huzzah!" everyone cheered.

Josiah moved next to Owen. "Good is taking place," he said, removing his glasses and looking around at the ballists. "Good will always triumph over evil." He cleared his throat. "And perhaps one day, evil will turn good again."

Ruby kissed the top of Uncle Owen's head and retrieved the baseball. She was about to slip it back into her pocket when Griffith stopped her.

"I'd like to hold it," he said.

"Why?" Ruby asked.

Griffith shrugged. "I just do."

"Try not to lose it." She placed the ball in his palm.

"I'll do my best."

*Sluggers*

Griffith looked to Truman, who had nestled up against his leg. Like so many times over the last several days, an ominous feeling surged through Griffith. He squeezed the baseball; his tight grip around the sphere seemed to ease his discomfort.

At least momentarily.

# 29

★

*The Attack*

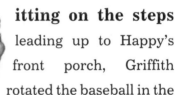

**itting on the steps** leading up to Happy's front porch, Griffith rotated the baseball in the palm of his hand and stared at Truman. He couldn't take his eyes off the hound, walking in *backward* circles around one of the great live oaks on the front lawn.

Ever since Griffith had taken the baseball from Ruby yesterday, Truman had been acting strangely. Last evening, during the team's low-key celebratory meal back at Happy's, he refused to enter the dining area. He sat outside in the foyer with his back to the festivities. After dinner, when some of the ballists from the Pelicans came over to toast their success, Truman had paced the porch like a night watchman. Overnight the hound had been equally unsettled. Several times Truman's whimpering had woken Griffith up, and the hound had insisted on sleeping (not that he slept much) facing the window and blocking the door. His erratic behavior, which even Preacher Wil found puzzling, continued this morning with the reverse pacing.

"Come on, boy," Griffith said, standing up and whistling for Truman. He stuffed the baseball into the front pocket of the shirt Uncle Owen had given him. "Let's go see if Ruby and Grams are almost ready to leave."

Because of Truman's restlessness, Griffith had awoken before everyone else. He had finished packing his belongings for the trip to

Charleston while the others were still in bed.

With Truman matching him step for step, Griffith headed through the house to Uncle Owen's room. To his surprise, his uncle and siblings were already packed up and ready for the train ride to South Carolina. Even more surprising was how alert and refreshed Uncle Owen appeared. Sitting up tall in his chair, he was in the middle of telling a story to Ruby and Graham, who were in front of him on the edge of his bed.

". . . the field was right by where our pop used to take us fishing every Sunday," he was saying. "Guy and I loved playing catch on that big open field. The best Sundays were the ones when your grandpa would hit us star chasers. He'd hit them as far as he could—and your grandpa was able to give the rock quite a ride in his day. We'd race after those sky balls and never have to worry about running into anyone or anything." Uncle Owen chuckled.

"Your father would do whatever was necessary to beat me to those balls—tackle me, trip me, grab hold of my clothes, you name it." He cleared his throat. "To this day, the great field at the bottom of Kiefer Hill is still my favorite place in all the world. Always brings to mind my brother, Guy."

Ruby rested a hand on Owen's leg and looked at Griffith. "Is everyone waiting for us?"

"Not yet," he replied. "They're all still upstairs. We might want to start helping Uncle Owen out front so that when they do finally make it—"

Suddenly the door to Uncle Owen's room burst open. Three of the Chancellor's men stormed in. One brandished a gun.

Truman leaped to his feet.

*Woof!*

The ferocious bark sounded more like a lion's roar, and every hair on the hound's back stood on end.

"No!" Ruby screamed.

"Get out!" Griffith yelled, jumping in front of his brother.

But the thugs weren't listening.

"Give us the baseball!" one of the goons barked, directing his words at Ruby and kicking the bedroom door shut.

"We're taking the boy!" shouted a second thug.

"Get him!" ordered the thug armed with the pistol.

As the two goons charged, Ruby grabbed hold of Graham, and Griffith raised his white-knuckled fists like a warrior. Barreling over Uncle Owen, one of the thugs lunged at Griffith, but before he could reach him, Truman leaped at the goon like a rabid dog and sank his teeth into the suited man's leg.

*Bang!*

A shot rang out.

The Chancellor's thug punched Truman's snout. As the hound loosened his grip, the goon kicked him away. Truman hit the wall by the bed, toppling the lamp on the end table and dislodging the mirror.

*Yelp! Yelp!*

Griffith dove at the other goon heading for his brother and sister.

*Bang! Bang!*

Wrapping his arms around the thug's frame and using every ounce of strength he had (and some he didn't know he possessed), Griffith *lifted* the goon off the ground and rammed him into the wall next to the door.

*Bang! Bang! Bang!*

The gunshots continued to echo in the small room, and as everyone dove for cover, it was impossible to determine if more shots were being fired or if the same bullets were ricocheting and reverberating off the walls.

Shaking on the floor by the bed, Ruby

shielded Graham with both arms, shut her eyes, and prayed. The Rough Riders *had* to have heard the commotion. They were on their way. At any moment, they would bust through the door and rescue them.

But Ruby knew the soldiers were upstairs. Chances were it would still take several more seconds—at least—for them to arrive. . . .

"No!" Ruby suddenly shrieked.

Several feet away was the most awful sight she had ever seen: Griffith lying motionless on the floor. Lying next to him, but slowly starting to move, was the thug Griffith had tackled. A small pool of blood covered the floor between them.

"Griff!" shouted Graham.

"No!" Ruby screamed again.

"Let's get out of here!" ordered the goon on his knees by the door, the smoke still rising from the barrel of his gun. "Come on!" He opened the door.

"We weren't supposed to shoot the kid!" the man who'd been attacked by Truman yelled. He scrambled up and raced to his dark-suited associate with the gun. "That was a direct order!"

"What about the ball and the other kid?" the third thug asked.

"There's no time!" shouted the armed goon, waving his weapon at the open door. "They're going to discover us any second!"

As quickly as they had burst in, the Chancellor's henchmen fled.

Too frightened to get up, Ruby and Graham crawled across the floor to Griffith, who still lay with his eyes closed.

"Griff!" Graham fought back tears as he shook his brother. "Wake up!"

"Say something!" Ruby pleaded, reaching for her brother's hand and squeezing her fingers.

To her surprise, Griffith squeezed them back.

"Griff!" Ruby screamed. "You're alive!"

Griffith managed a small smile. "I think so," he whispered, opening his eyes.

"Where are you hurt?" Graham asked. "They shot you!"

"I think not."

Without lifting his head, Griffith placed a hand over his chest. He reached into the pocket of his shirt—which now had a hole in the front—and pulled out the baseball.

"The baseball saved you!" Ruby

exclaimed, taking it from her brother. "The baseball stopped the bullet!"

"I think so," he whispered again.

Griffith winced as he struggled to sit up. Even though the baseball had protected him, he was still in pain from his fall and the force of the bullet hitting the ball.

His anxious eyes searched for Truman— and found him. The dog stood near the tipped-over table. When he saw Griffith look his way, he began to wag his tail. Truman hadn't been shot, only shaken up by the throw into the wall. The hound hobbled across the floor to the three Paynes and then licked Griffith's face.

"There's still only one hole in the ball," Graham noted. He took the sphere from Ruby and examined it more closely. "Wait a sec!" His eyes popped. "The new bullet entered the *same* hole!"

Griffith, Ruby, and Truman all leaned in. Just as Graham said, the fresh bullet had

bored into the baseball, but it didn't make a new hole. It had simply followed the same path that had already been blazed a year ago in Cuba.

"The baseball saved my life," Griffith said to his siblings. "Just like it saved Uncle Owen's."

As soon as Griffith said his name, all three looked to their uncle. He was hidden from view by his wheelchair, which had tipped over.

"Uncle O!" Graham shouted, speed-crawling across the bedroom floor.

Uncle Owen was still in his chair. His once-white shirt was covered in blood. So was the hardwood floor underneath and around his head. His eyes were closed. He wasn't moving.

"Uncle O!" Graham shook him like he had his brother a moment ago, though not nearly as hard. "Say something."

Uncle Owen didn't respond.

"No," Ruby sobbed. "Wake up."

"You can't die, Uncle Owen," said Griffith. "You can't."

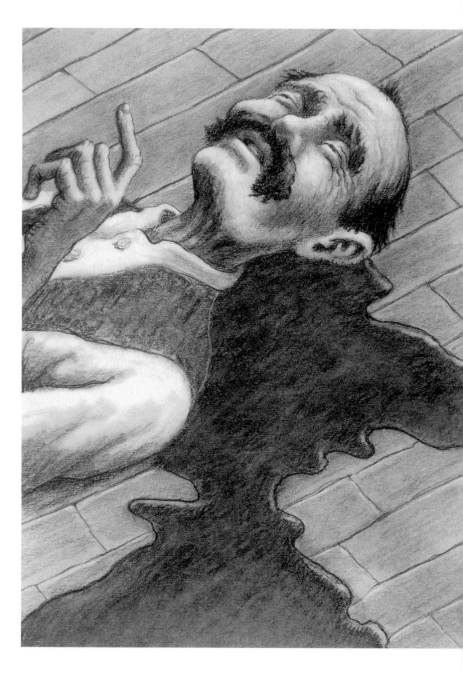

"What is it, Uncle O?"

Suddenly Uncle Owen's right arm began to move. Ever so slowly, he began to raise it in Ruby's direction. She leaned in so that his searching fingers could find her face. He then lowered them to her necklace, tracing his tips along the metal links until they reached the keys.

Uncle Owen's lips were moving, but no sounds were coming out.

"What is it, Uncle O?" Graham asked.

Griffith glanced to Truman. The hound's ears were perked, but instead of facing Uncle Owen, he was staring at the door.

The three Payne siblings inched forward. Uncle Owen gasped several times before uttering, "Tell Guy . . . tell Guy I had to. Tell him . . . I'm sorry. . . ."

The door to Uncle Owen's room swung open. But it wasn't Woody nor Scribe nor any of the Rough Riders bursting in. Rather, it was one of the Chancellor's goons, the one Griffith had tackled.

Griffith spun around and moved to dive in front of his brother and sister, but the sharp pain in his chest stopped him dead in his tracks. Griffith's eyes met Truman's. Struggling to his paws, the injured hound tried to block the thug's path, but the dark-suited man easily swatted the dog aside.

The thug tore across the room. However, instead of heading for Graham or Ruby, the dark-suited man charged at Griffith, barreling him over. The goon slammed Griffith's head into the floorboard and ripped the baseball from his hand. Scrambling to his feet, the thug shoved Ruby and Graham aside and then elbowed Truman in the neck. But instead of racing back into the hall—where more approaching footsteps could be heard—he ran full speed toward the large bedroom window.

Shattered glass flew about.

The Chancellor's man was gone. And so was the baseball.